Murder in the Mountains

WREN AND RASCAL COZY MYSTERY, BOOK 3

JUDITH A. BARRETT

WOBBLY CREEK, LLC

Murder in the Mountains

Wren and Rascal Cozy Mystery, Book 3

Published in the United States of America by Wobbly Creek, LLC

2023 Georgia

wobblycreek.com

Cover by Wobbly Creek, LLC

ISBN 978-1-953870-52-0 Ebook

ISBN 978-1-953870-53-7 Paperback

Dedication

Murder in the Mountains is dedicated to pink and turquoise and to stray and rescued dogs.

Previously

WREN

My name is Wren Weaver; I'm a freelance journalist and a camping enthusiast, so I was excited about the offer from a travel magazine publisher that combined my two passions. My assignment is to write about four haunted campgrounds across the United States and to provide feedback on the trailers we use for camping.

My constant companion is Rascal, my four-year-old black and tan Labrador Retriever, with a smidgeon of Husky. Our first assignment was at the Forgotten Oasis Campground in Hidden Gulch, Arizona. My publisher has my second article for the Lonesome Trail Campground in Dry Creek, Texas. Rascal and I are on our way to my third assignment: Bootleggers Creek Campground near the town of Dearheart in the mountains of Tennessee.

Rascal and I will return to Hidden Gulch after we complete our fourth haunted campground article. Even though we were in Hidden Gulch only a week, Marshal Justin Lewis and I became more than just friends; I'm excited that our relationship keeps growing stronger. Meanwhile, I miss him like crazy.

My publisher, Charlie Hogue, tried to play both sides of the fence when he hired a new editor. I later learned his editor was his nephew, Blake, my two-timing former friend from college. After Blake pulled his old trick of trying to insert himself into my writing, I made it clear to Charlie: accept my articles as written, or replace me. I'm fine either way.

When I was in college, I had very few friends because I was so focused on my studies; now I have good friends in Hidden Gulch, Arizona, and in Dry Creek, Texas, that I know I can count on, including at least three ghosts.

JUSTIN

I'm Justin Lewis, the marshal at Hidden Gulch. I came to Hidden Gulch three years ago and discovered the slow pace of a small town was what I needed to heal after I lost my wife in a car crash.

Before Wren and Rascal showed up, I thought I was immune to women, but Wren blasted that notion right out of my head the first time I saw her. When she gazed at me with her emerald green eyes and spoke to me in her soft, Georgia accent, she melted my heart that I thought had frozen long ago. She's petite and looks fragile, but that green-eyed beauty with light brown hair and its streaks of red that look like fire is absolutely fearless, and she terrifies me with the chances she takes.

She promised the Forgotten Oasis Campground ghost, Thomas, that she'd be back in six weeks, but I'm hoping it will be sooner. We're becoming closer every day, and the level of trust between us is growing; if I have my way, she'll be here permanently. I think she knows that, but maybe I should tell her.

Chapter One

Wren turned at the hand-crafted sign that proclaimed she had arrived at the Bootleggers Creek Campground; she lowered her window as she followed the gravel driveway a short distance through a stand of old pine trees.

She raised her eyebrows in wonder as she inspected the surroundings. "The ditch along the road has been mowed recently; so far, this is the best maintained campground we've seen."

When she reached a large log cabin with rocking chairs and oversized clay pots of colorful flowers on the wide, wraparound porch, she stopped at the sign that read, "Stop here for registration."

After she parked, she and Rascal strolled to the porch; Rascal flopped down to wait as Wren continued to the door.

Wren enjoyed the cool air and the refreshing aroma of pine mixed with citrus. She admired the welcoming atmosphere of the general store's décor: a potbelly stove, wooden rocking chairs with lap-sized quilts draped over the arms, and rough-hewn wooden shelves stocked for campers.

The middle-aged woman behind the desk peered at Wren over her glasses then frowned at her computer screen. "Do you have a reservation?"

"I'm Wren Weaver; my publisher told me he made a two-week reservation for me."

The woman narrowed her eyes as she continued to stare at her computer. "I don't see anything for Wren Weaver; could it be in another name?"

"His name is Charles Hogue."

She shook her head. "No, nothing here. Are you sure you're at the right campground?"

Wren pulled out her phone then found the text from Charlie. "I'm positive; I have a confirmation number."

The woman snorted. "That means he somehow made your reservation online; we discontinued our affiliation with that group two years ago. I'll have to check to see how he was able to do that; meanwhile, do you want to register? Did you say two weeks?"

"Can we register me for a week?"

"I'll need two days' notice if you're going to extend it."

"Okay, I'll know by next Tuesday if I can't wrap up in time to leave on Thursday morning."

The woman shrugged. "I'll need your vehicle tag number, your driver's license, and a credit card. You aren't a tent camper, are you? We don't have any tent sites left."

"I'm in a trailer, and I need a site with water and electricity."

"You have any pets?"

Wren nodded. "A dog."

"What breed?"

Do I even want to be here? "He's a Labrador Retriever."

The woman glared at Wren. "Any history of biting or being aggressive?"

"Not at all." Wren returned her glare. *Killers don't count.*

After the woman entered all of Wren's information and completed the financial transaction, she stapled Wren's receipt to a campground map. The woman picked up a permanent marker and used it to point to sections on the map. "This here's the ladies' restroom; the men's is on the opposite side of the building; this is the code to the restrooms and the Wi-Fi password."

She circled the code then drew a line under the password on the bottom of the sheet with the marker.

"The showers are in between the two restrooms. Each shower has a locking door, so we don't designate them as women's and men's."

The woman tapped on the map as she continued the map tour. "Pool, dumpster, dog park, and the trail to Bootleggers Creek."

She marked a square with an X. "This is your site. Chester will be here in just a minute to lead you to it, so you'll be parked the right way."

Wren peered at the X. "Looks like I'm pretty close to the women's restroom and the showers."

"You are." The woman flipped over the map. "These are our rules; they're just common sense but read them. If you need anything, the office is open from ten until five every day, except for Sundays, when we are closed."

She slipped the map into a folder with other papers then handed it to Wren. "In addition to the campground map, your folder has a history of the campground, a list of local attractions, and a list of businesses; the grocery store and gas station are probably the two you're most interested in. Dearheart is only two miles away."

The woman peered toward the front of the store. "He's out there now." She turned back to her computer and grumbled at the screen.

As Wren followed the golf cart, she said, "This campground is a huge contrast to our previous two campgrounds in more ways than one, Rascal. I definitely won't be interrupted by anyone dropping by to chat, but there's a trail we'll probably enjoy."

After Chester led Wren to her assigned campsite, he glowered at her then sneered as he sped away before Wren was in position to hook up to the utilities. She climbed out of the pickup to check her position.

She sighed. *I probably should be a little closer.*

She drove away from the site and around her row to approach the utilities on her left. She stopped then checked her position again.

"It's perfect, Rascal; I'm glad I had a little practice with the smaller trailer before we got here, or I would have stopped too far forward; backing up without a guide behind me is not my favorite thing to do."

Wren opened Rascal's door to let him out of the truck then plugged into the electrical outlet and attached the hose to the water faucet. She raised the back hatch of her teardrop trailer to make sure the gas connection to the burner was still tight.

"I wasn't sure if I'd like the outdoor kitchen, but so far, it's been fun," Wren said.

Rascal grinned.

"I'm glad the service manager in Waco took the time to show me how to dump the water; at least we're close to the bathroom, so maybe I can get by without needing to dump wastewater until we're ready to leave."

After Wren and Rascal went into the camper, she filled his water bowl.

While he drank, she said, "I'd like to check out the restrooms and showers; I'd rather shampoo my hair in the campground shower than use the extra water that I'll have to dump immediately because that canister for wastewater is so small." She pulled out her phone. "I'll snap a photo of the map, so I'll have the combination handy."

When they reached the building with the restrooms and showers, Rascal stayed outside while Wren went into the women's restroom. She smiled as she examined the soft yellow walls, the clean floors, and the sparkling sinks. "This is really nice."

Next, she went into a shower and admired the cleanliness of the terracotta walls and floor; after she inspected the large, open, tiled shower stall that had a built-in shelf for shower necessities and a shelf with hooks for towels and clothing next to it, she joined Rascal.

After they returned to the camper, Wren pulled out the list of businesses from the folder. "Let's go to the grocery store; I need something for supper, and we're out of eggs and cheese. I have one tortilla left to make a breakfast burrito."

Before they left, Wren jotted down a list of what she wanted from the store then sent a text to Justin. "We're here."

He immediately replied. "Is it a nice campground?"

"It's well-kept."

"T or c."

Wren smiled at his abbreviated message. *Text or call anytime.* She responded, "Thank you."

She sighed as she locked the camper then opened the pickup's back door for Rascal to hop inside.

Wren stopped at the gas station for fuel; while she refilled her tank, she glanced at the other customers who greeted one another as they filled their tanks or walked into or out of the store, but no one glanced toward her or attempted any eye contact.

After she returned the nozzle to its place, she climbed into her truck. "I wonder if I can write the article in three days, Rascal. Is it my imagination, or am I being completely ignored? I'll see how much online research I can do tonight then go to the library tomorrow for some local research."

Rascal stayed in the pickup while Wren hurried into the grocery store. She found prepackaged, ready to cook, single serving meals in grab-and-go sacks in the delicatessen area. *I can bake the chicken in my combo air fryer, toaster oven while I fry the potatoes and heat the green beans on the outdoor burner. I need ice cream.*

After she found the eggs and cheese, Wren beelined to the ice cream then hurried to the front to check out.

Wren was behind a woman who must have been related to the cashier because they chatted about ailments of people both of them knew.

After the woman left, the cashier quickly rang up Wren's purchases and put them into a sack then stared at the cash register screen until the sale was completed. She handed Wren the receipt and her sack then began ringing up the items of the customer behind Wren.

When Wren reached the pickup, she put her groceries on the passenger's seat and headed back to the campground.

On the way back to the campground, Wren said, "I feel so isolated, Rascal. There has to be something cultural going on that I don't understand."

While Rascal ate his supper, Wren called her mother.

"How are you and Rascal doing, honey?" Carolina asked. "Everything okay?"

"I'm in the mountains in Tennessee. The campground is beautiful, but it's totally weird; nobody's friendly at all."

"It's not you, Wren; I'll bet they've been a closed community for a lot of years, and they're leery of strangers."

"That must be it, Mom; I was certain I was invisible."

Carolina chuckled. "Not hardly; I have something that will cheer you up: Justin's mother called me. Her name is Ellen, but she goes by Ellie. We had a really pleasant chat."

Wren's eyes widened. "Mom, you didn't tell her anything embarrassing, did you?"

"Oh, you know me; of course, I did, but she told me stories about Justin too."

Wren smiled. "Will you tell me the stories?"

"Of course not; they were stories that only snoopy mothers would think are funny."

"Are you teasing me, Mom?" Wren furrowed her brow. *Please say yes.*

"Pretty much; Ellie did call me, but we didn't swap embarrassing stories. I thought you might like something to take your mind off the standoffish people you've seen today."

Wren giggled. "You did it, Mom. I must have run through at least twenty stories in my head that you absolutely must never repeat."

"Good, send me a list." Carolina laughed. "Thanks for calling, Wren; I was thrilled I could help."

"How did she get your phone number, Mom?"

"I called the Arizona campground and talked to Betsy, and she gave my number to Ellie."

Wren snorted. "Because you asked her to."

"One of my better ideas, don't you think?"

"I don't know, Mom; it depends on what kind of trouble you get me into."

"I'd never do that, sweetie; you do just fine by yourself. Talk to you later." Carolina laughed as she hung up.

I don't know if I should be worried or not. Wren sighed. "Rascal, I feel like I should start writing, but I have absolutely nothing to go on."

She glanced at the folder on her tiny table. "Unless our campground host has given us a gem. Didn't she say the folder had the history of the campground? I'll read after I eat or maybe while I eat."

Wren put the chicken that had been rolled in spices at the deli before it was packaged into the combination air fryer and toaster oven before she carried the potatoes and green beans to her outside kitchen.

Rascal stayed inside to guard the chicken as it air fried.

Wren opened the hatch door to her kitchen and pulled out a frying pan. While she stirred her potatoes and green beans in the pan, she watched as a newly arrived RV that was the size of a bus lumbered behind the golf cart in the row in front of her. When the RV passed her, the driver, an older man who wore a Texas State ball cap, glanced at her, and she raised her hand in a quick wave. He tapped the brim of his ball cap with his fingertips as he continued down the row.

Wren smiled as she stirred her potatoes and beans. *He's not from around here.*

After her potatoes were fried and her green beans had a little char on them, Wren served her vegetables onto a plate and closed the hatch before she went inside.

She inhaled the aroma of mingling spices and the chicken as she carried her plate into the camper. "Smells good in here, Rascal. I may have found a way to cook a delicious meal without a lot of prep."

Wren put her green, woven placemat on her small table then plated her chicken alongside the vegetables. When she cut off a piece of chicken and held it out for Rascal, he sat.

Rascal politely took the chicken from her fingers, then Wren cut a bite for herself. "Mmm, this is good."

After she finished eating, Wren put her dishes in the small dish pan she had bought two days ago. "So far, my small dish pan has worked out for me to wash and rinse my dishes in the laundry room and save water. Do you think I'm being too hyper about water conservation in the camper?"

Rascal sighed as he flopped down on the floor and closed his eyes.

Wren pulled out the folder to read the history of the campground and sat at her small table. When she was halfway through, Wren cheered as she jumped up from her seat and danced a jig; Rascal stared at her then joined into the celebration with a howl.

"This is outstanding, Rascal. We have our story. The short version is that the campground was the site of a bootlegger's still from the 1920s until the 1950s when the bootlegger's grandson died in a crash delivering a large order of moonshine to a customer. The bootlegger walked away from his lucrative operation and was never seen again. I'll write it up; we'll leave and be done. Let's go for a short walk then sit outside and enjoy the sunset until the bugs make us come inside for the evening. I'll take along my backpack and your leash for show, or in case we need it."

Wren pulled out her two camping chairs and set them up next to her trailer. She stood back to admire her camper and chairs. *Maybe this looks welcoming, so someone will stop for a chat.*

'Want to walk around, Rascal?"

While she and Rascal toured the campground sites, Wren gazed at the different styles of trailers and RVs. "How can a campground this inviting exist in a culture that is so aloof?"

A young woman in a truck two rows over from them waved as she parked next to a trailer. Wren smiled and returned the wave.

When Rascal grinned, the young woman said, "Hey there, boy. How are you doing?"

When Rascal bounded to her, Wren smiled as she followed him. *He's my social secretary.*

"Hi, I'm Dana Grace." The young woman smiled as she held out her hand.

"I'm Wren, and this is Rascal; nice to meet you."

After they shook hands, Dana Grace rubbed Rascal's face. "It's nice to see a friendly face; you must have come in this afternoon. Are you traveling?"

"Kind of, I'm here to write an article about the campground for a travel magazine; I expect to be here about a week. What about you?"

"I work at Jack's Apple Orchard Gift Shop; my uncle owns it. The woman who managed the gift shop for years retired and went to Florida to join her sister, so I'm here until he finds someone who can deal with his finicky ways, which is not me. How can I read your articles?"

"The travel magazine is printed for subscribers who prefer the traditional style of magazine that is usually sold in airports." Wren pulled out the small notebook from her backpack and scribbled the magazine's website. "They also have an online subscription service, and their website has samples of the articles. They've published my article about the Arizona campground."

"Thanks; I'm always looking for something new to read," Dana Grace said.

"How do you manage the large trailer by yourself?" Wren asked.

Dana Grace smiled. "I don't; the trailer belongs to my in-laws. My husband came with me to set it up, so I could help my uncle. My husband is away a lot with his job, so we're used to our nightly phone calls for weeks at a time. We're talking about getting our own fifth wheel, so I can tag along when he goes out of town. Being apart for most of the month gets old."

Wren smacked a feasting mosquito on her arm. "Time for us to go inside."

"Me too," Dana Grace said. "See you later, Rascal."

As they hurried back to the camper, Wren said, "That was exciting to meet someone who talked to us."

After they were in the camper, Wren opened her laptop to compose an email about the newest camper for Charlie and the CEO of the RV manufacturer. After she wrote her email, she read it aloud. "I love the twin bed, the small dining table and chair, the outdoor kitchen and its extra storage space, and the thermostat for air conditioning and heat. The big negative is no sewer hookup. I don't like removing the canister and dumping it at all. It's very heavy and messy."

Wren arranged the pillows on her bed, so she could write the next chapter of her "High Falutin' Killers" story in comfort.

Not long after sunset, her phone rang. *Betsy.*

"I'm so sorry I didn't have a chance to call you earlier, Wren, but it's kind of your fault because our business has really picked up since your article was published. Socorro asked me if I'd dress up as the Saloon Lady, and I told her I would if she'd ask Butch if he minded."

Wren laughed. "That squashed her plan, didn't it?"

"You got it; she tried to tell me I was an independent, grown woman who could do whatever I pleased and didn't need my husband's permission; when I asked her why she didn't dress up as the Saloon Lady, she hung up on me."

Wren laughed even harder.

"The reason I'm sorry I didn't call earlier is that your mother called me and asked me to give her cell number to Justin's mother. I don't know his mother, so I called the dispatcher, and she gave me the number. When I called Ellie, that's her name, and she's really nice, she was excited and told me she was calling your mother right away then hung up on me. Please don't hang up on me and don't tell Justin how I got his mother's number because the dispatcher called me back. She was crying and told me she'd breached confidentiality and shouldn't have given me the number, so I lied to her and told her I hadn't called and would tear up the number. I need you back here to keep me from being the one getting into trouble."

Wren smiled. "Because I'm the one that gets into trouble?"

Betsy exhaled. "Exactly; I knew you'd understand. So, where are you now?"

"I'm at the Bootleggers Creek Campground."

"That's in the mountains of Tennessee, right? Is it nice? Do they have a saloon?"

"No saloon; the campground is beautiful."

"Send me a picture; maybe I'll get some ideas for us."

"I'll take a photo in the morning, but I'm not sure how useful it will be. The annual rainfall here is around fifty inches, and your annual rainfall is like ten inches."

"Wow; do you have a camper that will float? Doesn't the creek flood? How did you know what the annual rainfall is there? Did you make it up? It's okay if you did."

"I learned in Texas that I want to understand the local weather, so I researched it. The creek does flood, but not very often."

"I have to hang up; I'm an independent woman who needs to have supper ready for that man who would back me up if I told Socorro he said I couldn't dress like the Saloon Lady."

"Thanks for calling."

After they hung up, Wren said, "I miss Betsy, Rascal; we need to be in the same time zone."

Rascal nosed the door; Wren put on her boots and sprayed mosquito repellent on her arms then smeared some on her face before they went outside.

While Rascal wandered around their campsite, Wren gazed at the sliver of a moon and the clear sky. *So many stars; not much light pollution here at all.*

She glanced around the campground and shook her head. *It's almost full.*

Rascal trotted to the door, and they went inside.

Wren checked the time. "I have plenty of time for a shower."

She gathered her shower things. "You can stay here if you like, Rascal. There may not be a shower available anyway, with all the RVs that are here."

Rascal followed her out the door.

When she reached the shower closest to her camper, Wren raised her eyebrows. "This one is available; maybe I'm the only one who won't take a shower in their rig."

Wren skipped shampooing; after she soaped up then rinsed, she quickly dried and dressed. While they were walking back to her camper, Wren stopped to listen to the roar of a racing engine.

"Sounds like it's behind the campground, doesn't it?" She listened for a few minutes; the abrupt silence was almost as startling as the sudden noise of the engine.

After they were inside, Wren put her waistband holder in place and slipped in her carry pistol. She picked up her laptop but set it down before she began her next chapter. "Rascal, there's not enough in the campground history for me to write my article. It sounds good on the surface, but on a closer look, it really says very little."

Her phone rang; she smiled as she answered it before the second ring.

"You're calling early, aren't you?"

Justin chuckled. "For a change, I'm calling at a normal time instead of late. I had a routine day, which was great. How about you?"

Wren sighed. "I don't know why the campground made Charlie's list of those that are haunted. My registration folder included a one-page history of the campground. Can I read it to you?"

"I'd love to listen to you read; go right ahead."

After Wren read it, Justin said, "It has some holes, doesn't it?"

"Exactly; at first, I thought it was great because I could write my article from the information I had, but then I thought of so many questions. Do you think the grandson's crash was an accident?"

"I wouldn't think an experienced driver like a bootlegger would have suddenly driven off the road unless the weather or road conditions were poor, but wouldn't that have been included in the history?" Justin asked.

"Yes, bad weather would be a logical explanation; maybe the grandfather begged his grandson not to go out in the heavy rain or snowstorm, but the grandson didn't want to let the family down. That would have made a great story, but there's nothing."

"Following up on that, I can't help but wonder why the old man walked away. We don't know whether it was guilt, family pressure, or something more sinister," Justin said.

"It looks like a simple, straight-forward story, but it just has so many holes." Wren furrowed her brow as she stared at the sheet. "Now, I wonder who wrote it and why. Maybe that's something I can ask."

"So, what's your plan for tomorrow?"

"I couldn't find anything online, so I thought I'd go to the local library."

"Maybe the librarian will know who wrote the article or why the campground is considered haunted," Justin said.

"That's what I'm hoping." Wren smiled. "I knew you'd see how the article brought up more questions than answers."

"Which reminds me, did you know my mother called yours?" Justin asked.

"I called Mom earlier, and she told me, but she didn't share any details at all. Do you know what that's all about?"

"Not a clue; I think I'll call Dad to see what he knows."

"That's a good idea; I'll check with my dad too."

"Tell me more about the campground and the people you've met; I want to hear more about your day," Justin said.

"The people are really standoffish; Mom said it's because they've been isolated for so many years."

"Back in the day, I suspect every family around there had at least one bootlegger cooking moonshine in the woods somewhere, so there would have been an unspoken rule about keeping your mouth shut, especially around strangers who might be the law. Originally, the Bureau of Alcohol, Tobacco, and Firearms was under the Internal Revenue Service, which is why the agents who broke up stills and arrested moonshiners were called Revenuers."

"So, why did local sheriffs bust up stills? They weren't part of the ATF," Wren said.

"In the 1920s, sheriffs were paid ten dollars for destroying a still and an extra fifty dollars for catching a moonshiner; you've hit my area of expertise, honey."

"That was a lot of money back then."

"How's it going for you with that outdoor kitchen?" Justin asked.

"So far, I love it because of the extra storage and counter space. Speaking of campers, I met a young woman this evening who was friendly; she's staying in her in-laws' large trailer while she works at her uncle's gift shop. Her husband travels, and they've talked about getting a fifth wheel, so she can travel with him," Wren said.

"It seems to me that you aren't running into all that many solos that are camping while they travel."

"That's true; all the singles I've seen are permanent or semi-permanent like Dana Grace."

"That's interesting that Dana Grace and her husband are talking about a fifth wheel rather than a self-contained RV."

"I kind of understand it. The large RVs seem a little awkward as they maneuver through the campgrounds, and the fifth wheels seem to be more stable than the trailers."

"After your assignment is completed, do you think you'll have your fill of camping?" Justin asked.

"Not at all, except I'd want to go camping on a weekend or a brief vacation and not be working."

"It's getting late there, isn't it?"

Wren stifled a yawn. "A little, but I love talking to you."

"I love you, Wren."

Wren's mouth stayed open. *What do I say? I love you too doesn't sound sincere at all.*

Justin cleared his throat. "Are you mad at me? Did I ruin everything? I'm really sorry; I can make it a little more light-hearted, if that would help. Wren?"

"I've been afraid to say anything because I was afraid I'd scare you away. I love you so much."

"I'll always love you, Wren."

"So, how were you going to make it a little more light-hearted?"

"I don't know; that was a desperate attempt to backtrack, so you wouldn't hate me forever."

"How about if I love you forever instead?"

"Sealed with a kiss?" Justin asked.

Wren giggled. "Absolutely."

"Send me another selfie tomorrow, so I can see what it's like around you. I think about you all the time, Wren; you owe me an I love you kiss, you know."

"I like the sound of that. If I can't learn anything tomorrow that will help me write my article, I'll throw together some words like the history of the campground sheet, send it to Charlie, and tell him to have Blake finish it up while I go to the next assignment."

"Now I'm hoping you don't come up with anything at all." Justin chuckled.

"I really like the idea of tossing this story over the fence."

"But you won't; I'll talk to you tomorrow."

After they hung up, Wren and Rascal went outside for his bedtime break. A few clouds had moved in; the cicadas were buzzing, and the katydids added to the fracas. "We might have some rain tonight according to the bugs, Rascal."

While Wren gazed at the different styles of trailers and campers around their site, Rascal gave a low growl, and his hackles raised as he faced the end of the row in front of them. Wren peered in the direction of Rascal's alert and realized that Chester sat in his parked golf cart in the shadows. *He's watching the Texas Tech guy's rig.*

When Wren rose to fold up her camping chairs, she noticed Chester was still parked in the same position. After Wren and Rascal went into the camper, she changed into her favorite dark blue pajamas with the cute yellow baby ducks and turned off the lights. She sat next to the window as she watched the lights go out in the RVs and trailers across the campground.

Her phone buzzed a text from Justin. "t or c. ly."

She smiled and replied, "ly 2."

When the campground was dark except for the subdued glow of the security light, she pulled down the blind then climbed into bed and fell asleep to the sound of a roaring engine.

Chapter Two

Wren woke before daylight to the din of a downpour accompanied by wind gusts that rocked her camper. She pulled her pillow over her head, but the rain continued its incessant drumming on her roof while her bed shook with each wind blast. She peeked out from under her pillow at the microwave to check the time, but it was flashing. *Coffee maker is flashing too.*

"I guess we had an outage sometime last night." Wren hugged her pillow as she checked her phone then groaned. "Five o'clock is too early for me, but I won't be able to sleep in the storm."

She set the time on her coffee maker and started it brewing before she set the time on the microwave.

Rascal waited at the door; Wren opened it, and he dashed outside. While Wren held the door open, the wind switched directions, and the rain soaked her and her pajamas. When Rascal returned, she grabbed a towel and rubbed him down before he shook himself to dry.

"While the coffee perks, I'll run to the restroom. I can't get any wetter than I am."

Wren slipped on her flip flops then clutched her phone in her hand as she dashed out of the camper toward the restroom. The pale orange glow from the security light gave an eerie cast to the campground and was completely useless for seeing what was ahead in the heavy rain. She sped up as the rain intensified, and in her rush, Wren tripped over a large obstruction on the ground and flew across the wet leaves and soggy ground before she landed in a face plant. *At least I had a death grip on my phone and didn't lose it.*

She groaned as she rose then limped barefooted to the restroom.

She checked her phone for the code. *I resisted memorizing the code, but I guess I better do it after all.*

After she used the restroom and cleaned the mud and leaves from her face, hands and arms, Wren turned on her phone's flashlight. *Should have used it in the first place, but I didn't expect a tree to be down.*

She stepped gingerly on her left foot with its twisted ankle and flinched when she stepped on rocks and sticks as she made her way back to her camper. *I hope I can find my flip flops; I need a walking stick.*

She stopped for a moment to gather her reserves then ducked her head and continued moving.

I am completely drenched. Tears mixed with the rain on her face as she winced and watched for the log that had tripped her. When she neared it, she squinted at the object. *That's not a log.*

When she was closer, she stifled a scream as she recognized the man lying on his back with a bright red hole in the middle of his forehead. His arms were outflung; near his right hand was a Texas State ball cap.

In her panic, Wren fumbled with her phone as she turned off her flashlight, so the killer that she was certain lurked under the cover of the black night and driving rain couldn't see her. She ran to her camper at a speed fueled by the terror that gripped her far worse than the pain in her ankle or the fresh cuts and bruises on the bottoms of her feet. When she reached her camper, she dashed inside and called Justin.

When he answered on the second ring, he was groggy.

"What's wrong, Wren?" he mumbled.

"I fell over a dead body on my way to the campground bathroom, but I didn't know it was a body until I was on the way back."

Justin's voice was clear as he asked, "Where are you?"

"I'm in my camper; I ran because I was scared the killer might still be around."

"Lock the door; call nine-one-one then call me back."

Wren called nine-one-one.

When the dispatcher answered, Wren said, "I'm at the Bootleggers Creek Campground and found the body of a man on my way back from the restroom."

"Are you safe?"

Wren sighed with relief at the concern in the man's kind voice.

"Yes, I ran to my camper and locked the door; my dog is with me."

After he asked her name, phone number, and site number, the dispatcher said, "We'll get someone right there. Stay inside; they'll come to your site."

When she hung up, Wren immediately called Justin. Her teeth began chattering as he answered.

"Wren, are you okay?"

"I twisted my ankle and lost my flip flops when I fell over the body of a man who had been murdered; I have cuts on the bottom of my feet, and there's blood all over the floor. I got drenched in the rain, and I'm freezing; my baby duck pajamas are soaked," she sobbed.

"Strip down, honey, and dry off; put on some warm clothes, but don't hang up. Put me on speakerphone. Did you say you fell over a body?"

"I fell on my way to the restroom, but I didn't know what tripped me until I was on the way back to my camper."

"Did you have your carry piece? Is it wet?"

Tears streamed down Wren's face. "I didn't have it because I went to the restroom in my pajamas." She wailed. "The killer could have been right next to me."

"Easy, Wren; you're okay," Justin whispered. "Rascal's with you. You're safe, honey."

As Justin continued to comfort Wren, she slowly relaxed.

She shivered. "Thank you so much for understanding. I'd better change; I'm cold."

Wren went into her small bathroom and quickly stripped off her pajamas before she rubbed her hair with a bath towel then wrapped it around her head. She put her feet in her dishpan and poured a bottle of water over her feet to rinse the dirt and blood away. She dried her feet with paper towels then grabbed another bath towel and dried herself.

"Are you doing okay, Wren?"

"Much better; I'm almost dry. The night air is chilly, but not cold enough for the heater to kick in; I was freezing."

"Put on some warm clothes or send me a selfie."

"Justin!"

He chuckled. "Just checking to see if you were listening."

After she put on a pair of sweatpants, a T-shirt, a sweatshirt, and a pair of dry socks, she stuck her waistband holster inside her sweatpants then added her pistol. She raised her eyebrows when Justin mumbled, "Didn't get my photo."

After she removed the towel from her head, she glanced in the mirror. *I'm a mess.*

Wren took a selfie and sent it to Justin. "I put on warm clothes and sent you a selfie."

He said, "Wrong order."

When Wren giggled, Justin said, "I was hoping you'd take that in the spirit it was intended."

"I understood you perfectly, didn't I?"

When Wren received a short video of Justin trying to look aggrieved and innocent, she giggled. "Thank you, honey; I feel much better."

Wren exhaled before she continued, "I recognized the man; I don't know his name, but he was an older man who had arrived at the campground late yesterday. He wore a Texas State ball cap, drove a large bus-style RV with a towed; both vehicles had Texas license plates."

"When you say he had a toad, you mean he towed a vehicle?" Justin asked.

"That's RV talk. A towed is a towed vehicle, but you'll see it spelled like the amphibian toad in a lot of RV articles."

"We need to go camping," Justin said, "but I don't think we want an RV with a toad."

"No, I think we'd like a fifth wheel."

Wren heard the crunch of tires as a car stopped in front of her trailer. "I think the local law is here; the dispatcher said they'd come to my site."

"Okay, honey; call me later."

"I will; sorry I woke you, but I knew it would be okay."

"It was; I love you, sweetheart, and thank you for the selfie."

Rascal growled as he faced the door. Wren lifted a slat in the window blind to peer outside.

"I think he might be a state trooper, but his car is not marked. I'll wait until he knocks; that rain hasn't slowed down at all."

When the trooper knocked, Wren opened the door and raised her eyebrows at the tall man who wore rain gear over his state police uniform.

"Miss Weaver? I'm Trooper Benson with the Tennessee State Police."

"I'd invite you in, but you wouldn't be able to stand up in here."

Trooper Benson peered inside her camper and chuckled. "I don't think I could even sit up straight."

The state trooper held out his hand for Rascal, but Rascal positioned himself between Wren and the trooper and backed up against Wren.

"This is Rascal," Wren said.

"How did you find the body? Was Rascal with you?"

"No, I was running to the restroom in the rain, but it was raining so hard, I was almost blinded. I fell over something that I thought was a log, but I didn't stop to check. On my way back, I had to move slower because I'd twisted my ankle, and that's when I found the body."

"Where was the body?" he asked.

"It's between here and the restrooms; I think it was on the other side of the road that goes past my row."

"Do you have an umbrella?" he asked.

"No, I don't, but I will later today."

"Good plan; I'll be right back."

Trooper Benson returned with an umbrella. "Can you show me where the body is?" he asked.

Wren swallowed hard then slipped on her boots. "Yes, sir."

When Rascal headed toward the door, Wren said, "Stay, Rascal; there's no reason for you to get wet again. I'll be fine."

Rascal quietly growled then flopped down on the floor.

When Wren grimaced as she stepped out of her camper, Trooper Ben said, "Let's take the cruiser, so you don't have to walk the whole way there on that ankle."

He opened the passenger door for Wren. After she was inside, he hurried to the driver's side.

"Was he off the road?" he asked.

"I'm pretty sure he was because when I fell, the ground was soft and soggy, not hard or with puddles like it would be from being compacted by vehicles driving on it."

Trooper Benson stopped on the road that was close to the restrooms. "Around here? Can you show me?"

He opened the door for her and helped her climb out. After she opened the umbrella, Wren slowly limped toward the restrooms while the trooper swept the area with his flashlight.

"There's his Texas State ball cap." Wren pointed. "Oh, and there's one of my flip flops."

"How far from the body was the cap?" Trooper Benson asked.

"His arms were spread out, and he was practically touching it with his right hand."

"I'll take you back to your camper, then I'll look around before I call for help. If you think of anything else, here's my card with my cell phone number."

Wren took his card and picked up her flip flop but didn't see the second one.

After Wren was back in her camper, she poured a cup of coffee and sighed. *I'll let Justin sleep.*

After she finished her second cup of coffee, Wren opened her laptop to write the next chapter of "High Falutin' Killers".

An hour later, her concentration was broken when her stomach rumbled, and Rascal whined. She glanced at the time on the microwave. "You're ready for breakfast, aren't you? So am I."

When Wren pulled out his food from the cabinet then dished it up, Rascal danced.

"It's past our usual time for breakfast, and I'm starving."

While he ate, she opened the blinds then stared through the rain at the flashing red lights between her camper and the restrooms.

"Looks like the rain hasn't let up at all, and Trooper Benson got his help, but I'm not sure that means he didn't find the body, or he did."

She opened the weather app on her phone and sighed. "It's going to rain all day."

Wren picked up the information sheet to see if there were any nearby diners. "I'm suddenly not as enamored with the outdoor kitchen as I have been. The Copper Kettle Diner isn't far from the gas station and looks promising; by the time I buy an umbrella, look for flip flops, a walking stick, and maybe a rain jacket, and have breakfast, the library will probably be open. You'd have to spend most of the morning in the truck. Do you want to go or stay?"

Rascal trotted to the door.

"I thought so, but I wanted to ask."

Wren slipped her laptop into her backpack and picked up her keys. "I should let Justin know what happened, but I know what he's going to say, and I don't want to start an argument. He's probably getting ready for work; I'll just send him a quick text."

She frowned at her phone. "If I send him a text that the body's missing, he'll call me right away; I might as well call him."

Justin answered before the second ring ended. "You caught me at a good time. I just pulled into the parking lot; my first meeting of the day doesn't start for another hour, but I came in early to get some work done for a change. How are you doing?"

"A state trooper asked me to show him the body, but all we found was the Texas State ball cap."

"What? Wasn't that less than twenty minutes after you fell over the dead man? I don't like this at all. The killer must have seen you when you came out of your camper then hid until you returned to it. Wren, I really wish you'd leave there right away."

"I knew you'd be worried, but the campground is crawling with law enforcement; I'll be safe here while I write my article. If I can learn why the campground is considered haunted, I'll have enough to write my article. I'm going to the local diner for breakfast then the library, and Rascal's going with me. I'm certain I'll pick up enough local lore, so I can write my article and leave as soon as possible."

Justin sighed. "Will you pay attention to Rascal?"

"I will; I tend to keep bad news to myself, but I don't want there to be any walls between us."

"You say it better than I could, but I'm the same."

After they hung up, Wren said, "That was hard, but I'm glad I called him; let's go."

When Wren reached the campground exit, a sheriff's deputy stopped her; she lowered her window.

"Excuse me, ma'am; do you mind if I take a quick look in your backseat?" He peered past her. *He's making sure no one's hiding in my truck.*

Wren lowered the back window. "Go right ahead."

Rascal greeted the deputy at the window as he shined his flashlight in the back seat.

The deputy chuckled as he held out his hand for Rascal to smell. "Good boy."

The deputy strode to the back of her truck and examined the truck bed then returned to her door and waved her on. "There's standing water on the roads; be safe."

Wren stayed well under the speed limit as she headed toward the gas station with her wipers set to their highest setting.

When she hit a deep puddle on the side of a winding road that had a steep drop off, her steering wheel jerked as the force of the water abruptly thrust her tires sideways. Wren tightened her clutch on the steering wheel and resisted the urge to overcorrect as she straightened her tires; she continued to maintain her tight grip on the steering wheel as she slowed her speed even more for the rest of the way to the gas station.

Wren exhaled in relief as she parked as close to the front door of the gas station store as she could. "That was scary. Justin told me before we left Texas that he was worried about the winding roads in the mountains; now I understand what he was talking about, but he doesn't need to hear that."

Before Wren climbed out of the truck, she said, "I won't be long."

She ran from the truck to the door but still dripped on the floor when she rushed through the door.

"Goodness, honey. I hope you're here for an umbrella." The middle-aged cashier with shockingly red hair from a bottle, bright red circles on her cheeks, and penciled-in, high-arched eyebrows smiled.

Wren returned her smile. "You guessed it."

"Where y'all from, honey? You sound like a Georgia girl."

Wren's eyes widened. "I am; you must have a good ear for accents."

"Lord, no; my sister married a Georgia farmer thirty years ago, and you sound exactly like her. Do you know her? She's a Williams now; maybe you know her husband's people."

"I'm not sure; my mama would, though."

"You tell your mama to tell my sister hey for me; she'll get a kick out of that."

Wren nodded then glanced around.

"Them umbrellas are in aisle two. We have ponchos too, but they're cheap plastic and won't last. There's a hiking store in town; they've got some sturdy gear. Get yourself a nice rain jacket that will last you for years."

"Thanks, I'll do that; what about flip flops? I lost one of mine."

"We got you covered there; we have the plainest, cheapest flip flops you can find outside of Florida. They won't last long, but you could buy three pairs and still not pay close to what a fancy pair would cost you. Aisle four for them; holler if you can't find what you want, and I'll help you."

Wren started at aisle two and chose a bright turquoise and dark green umbrella; in aisle four, she selected a pair of hot pink flip flops because they were the only ones that she could find in her size.

When she set her items next to the cash register, the cashier smiled. "You've got yourself a right colorful selection here, honey."

"I do, don't I? I must be trying to make up for the gloomy skies."

"Sounds like a good plan to me. I'll put your flip flops into a bag with your receipt for you."

As the cashier rang up the sale, Wren asked. "Where's the best place to get a good breakfast?"

"Cooper Kettle's just down the road; you can't miss it. Be sure to get a biscuit and ask for jam from the kitchen; it's home canned by the ladies around here during berry season. They have that commercial jelly on the table for people not from around here, but you don't want that."

After the cashier handed Wren a plastic bag with the flip flops and the receipt inside, she asked, "Is that your dog in your truck? He has a sweet face. He coulda come in with you; bring him in next time."

"Thanks, I will; he enjoys being around people."

"Be safe on those roads, honey. Some of them hairpin turns come up on you sudden like."

"I will. Thank you." Wren stepped outside and opened her umbrella.

Chapter Three

Wren dashed to her truck. "The cashier said you can go with me into the store. That's nice to know."

After she pulled onto the road toward the Copper Kettle Diner, Wren said, "She told me to ask for kitchen jam at the diner, which is homemade jam and to go to a hiking gear store for a rain jacket; I feel like a local after talking to her."

When Wren pulled into the parking lot at the Copper Kettle Diner, her eyes widened at the number of pickup trucks and cars. "We might have to come back later, Rascal; I don't see a place to park."

She drove slowly around the lot. Two young men came out of the diner; as they rushed to their truck, one of the men waved for Wren to follow them. When he pointed at a truck a few vehicles away, she stopped and waited for them to back out. After they pulled away, they waved, and she honked in appreciation as she took their parking spot.

"People are nice here after all: just not all of them."

Rascal grinned then flopped down on the back seat for a nap.

The diner was as packed as the parking lot. She stood in the back of a long line that snaked from the entrance to the cash register as it blocked the main aisle. A young woman with a full coffeepot in her hand cut through the line to breeze past her and whispered, "Go stand at the far end of the counter near the ladies' room; a couple of men are getting ready to leave."

Wren excused herself as she made her way past the people in line then headed toward the ladies' room. While she stood near the door and tried to look casual and inconspicuous, a man motioned for her to move closer to the counter.

When she did, he rose, "Here you go; nice seeing you."

She sat at his seat as he headed toward the door.

The man next to her nudged her. "We look after our own. You're related to that Williams family in Georgia, I hear."

"On my mama's side," she mumbled.

"Coffee?" the young woman asked. "Do you need a menu, or are you ready to order?"

"Coffee's great; I'd like a fried egg, bacon, biscuit, and kitchen jam."

"You got it, girlfriend."

The young woman pulled out a coffee cup from under the counter and filled it then rushed to the order window. "Grill me a single squealer from the kitchen."

When her breakfast came, Wren's eyes widened at the size of the biscuit that sat next to her perfectly fried egg and three slices of thick bacon. The young woman placed a small bowl with a dollop of butter and a second bowl with a generous serving of strawberry jam. *I won't have to eat until suppertime.*

Wren split her biscuit then buttered each half before she scooped up jam with her spoon and heavily covered both halves of her biscuit. She pulled several napkins from the paper napkin holder on the counter and put two slices of bacon on them then dug into her breakfast.

After she ate her egg, one piece of bacon, and half of her biscuit, she gazed longingly at her other half.

The young woman giggled as she dropped a small to-go carton in front of Wren's plate. "I can't eat the entire biscuit either. Who's the bacon for?"

Wren smiled. "My dog's waiting for me in my truck. He'll enjoy the treat."

"Next time you come, be sure to go to the ladies' room and wash your hands first thing." The young woman winked.

"I'll do that, thanks."

After Wren packaged her biscuit and bacon, the man next to her said, "One second; my brother just came in."

Wren nodded as she pulled out her money for a tip; when a man stood behind her, she set down her tip next to her plate and slid off her stool.

"Thanks," the man who stood behind her said. "See you tomorrow; tell your mama hey from me."

Wren nodded. *Tennessee's not so bad, after all.*

She stepped outside and smiled. *No rain.*

As she headed toward her pickup, a young couple in a truck pulled into the parking lot. The young woman waved, and Wren motioned for them to follow her. *I'm a local.*

After she pulled away, they pulled into her parking spot.

On her way to town, Wren said, "I saw a dog park on the list of town attractions. I'll see if I can find it from the directions. I have the sheet in my backpack."

Wren parked in the grocery store parking lot and gave Rascal a slice of bacon before she pulled out the information sheet.

"It looks like it's only two blocks from here."

After they arrived at the dog park, Wren said, "No one's around; they probably changed plans with all the rain. My feet are pretty sore, so I don't think I could do the trail through the woods today, but you can explore to see what you think about it."

After they were inside the gate for the dog park, Wren sat on the wooden bench while Rascal investigated the park and checked the trees for squirrels.

Wren relaxed in the gentle breeze. When her phone buzzed with a text from Justin, she smiled as she read it.

"I checked your weather; it's supposed to clear up sometime this morning. How are you doing?"

He didn't say call.

She responded with a text. "Relaxing at the dog park while Rascal searches for squirrels. Clear, blue skies with a gentle breeze and no bugs."

"You're not at the campground?"

Wren bit her lip. *He's worried.* "I bought an umbrella and had a delicious breakfast at the Copper Kettle Diner."

Wren's phone rang.

"Hi, honey," she said. "I thought you couldn't talk."

Wren held her breath. *How mad is he?*

"I couldn't because I was in a meeting; I had to step out into the hall and laugh, so I called you. Did you know that copper is the pot of choice for cooking moonshine because it has antibacterial properties that remove sulfur created by yeast during fermentation? The copper makes a higher quality moonshine that is smoother and has a pleasant aroma."

Wren giggled. "No, that's hilarious."

"I loved the play on words; can you imagine back in the day when the city guys from the ATF showed up intending to find stills then sat at the counter and ate breakfast with the county's most successful and probably richest moonshiners?"

"You have a strange sense of humor for a lawman."

"I just love history; there's so much to learn from the old days."

"You have a minute for a story?"

"Sure do."

Wren told him about the cashier at the gas station and her sister from Georgia; when she added her mama might know the family, Justin laughed.

"How long did it take to get around that you're related to the sister from Georgia?"

"Less than ten minutes."

She told him about the diner, the waitress, and the man telling her he heard she was related to the Williams family in Georgia.

He laughed even harder. "On your mama's side, am I right? You're a local and deserve a place at the counter. I'm proud of you, honey. The bonus is that you have the entire county watching your back."

"I didn't think of that."

"Maybe not consciously, but well played; I have to go. Thanks for the break; love you and your stories."

After they hung up, Wren smiled. *We definitely don't see things the same; interesting balance, and I'm glad he wasn't mad.*

Rascal trotted to her with his tongue hanging out.

"Let's fill your water bowl, so you can have a drink, then we'll go by the library to see what their hours are before I look for a rain jacket."

After Rascal had his fill, they went to the library. Wren parked in the empty lot near the front door; she and Rascal hopped out to read the signs on the door.

"They open at ten, so we'll have plenty of time to shop for a rain jacket and a walking stick. The other sign says that pets are welcome here. There has to be a story."

Wren parked on the street near the hiking store; Rascal waited outside the store while she went inside.

A slim, elderly man greeted Wren. "Did you want to browse, or were you looking for something?" He smiled. "I need to know if I should stay out of your way or if I can ask you if you need any help."

Wren returned his smile. "I need a rain jacket and a walking stick."

He nodded. "Twisted your ankle?"

"Yes, sir, and got a few cuts on my feet running barefooted."

"Ouch. Let's start with the walking stick. We have hiking sticks and trekking poles. The trekking poles come in pairs, so I think one of our great hiking sticks will double as a walking stick for you while you give your ankle and feet a chance to heal. Your dog can come inside, if you like; we're an outdoor store and love hiking companions."

He pointed to the shoe section and the four chairs. "Sit there, and I'll bring you two or three hiking sticks that are right for you. You can pick the style and wood you like."

Wren opened the shop's door. "You're invited inside, Rascal."

Rascal followed Wren to the chairs and laid next to her chair when she sat down.

The man returned with three hiking staffs. "We have hickory, maple, and aluminum."

After Wren stood, she walked with each one with Rascal at her side. "The aluminum is lighter, but I love the feel of the hickory and love the leather strap."

"I could tell by the way you walked with it." The man smiled. "Let's get you a rain jacket. Something lightweight is your best bet, but it needs to be roomy enough, so you can layer under it. Do you have a color preference?"

"Not at all; I'm more into serviceable than fashion."

"In that case, I've got the perfect jacket for you, and rather than a hood, I suggest you might like a wide-brimmed hat that will keep the rain out of your eyes and the back of your neck dry. The hat also doubles as a sun hat. Bring your hiking stick, and I'll show you."

After Wren tried on a jacket, the man narrowed his eyes.

"That may be the right size for you. Let's try one size larger, but I'm afraid the sleeves will be too long."

"How does it feel?" he asked after she switched jackets.

"Too big."

"I agree. Put on the one we like, and I'll pick out a hat for you. Pink or turquoise?"

Match my umbrella or my flip flops? "Turquoise."

He went to the next aisle then returned with a hat that had a turquoise brim and a gray top.

Wren put on the hat and modeled her hat, jacket, and stick in front of a full-length mirror. "This is perfect."

"Anything else?" the man asked. "If you planned to go hiking in the mountains, I'd suggest hiking boots, but we'll wait on that until your ankle heals. I do have a backpack that would be the perfect size for your rain gear. Do you have an umbrella with you? It also has a slot for an umbrella."

"That sounds interesting."

"Is your umbrella in your truck? Why don't you bring it in, and we'll see if the backpack will work for your gear."

Wren used her new staff to walk to her pickup then returned with her umbrella and Rascal still at her side.

The elderly man slipped her umbrella into a pouch on the side of the backpack then closed a strap around it. "What do you think?"

"I like it." After Wren paid for her items, she and Rascal headed for the library.

"You know that since I have an umbrella, rain jacket, and hat, we won't see any rain ever again, don't you?" Wren chuckled.

Rascal yipped.

The first row of parking spots closest to the library was filled when they arrived.

"Popular place." Wren opened the back door for Rascal after she parked in the second row.

When she walked into the library, the sound of lively conversations reminded her of the library in Hidden Gulch, and a tear escaped and slipped down her cheek.

"Allergies?" The short, round, older woman behind the desk peered at Wren through red-framed glasses with thick lenses that magnified her hazel eyes. Her gray, wispy hair had streaks of bright blue that surrounded her face.

Wren smiled. "Must be."

"They're always worse after a rain, aren't they? Can I help you find something?"

"I'm writing an article for a travel magazine about campgrounds that are reported to be haunted. I have the write-up from Bootleggers Creek Campground, but it mentions nothing about being haunted."

The woman tittered. "It wouldn't. I'll introduce you to someone who can fill you in on the legend that some swear is fact, and others claim is gossip bordering on slander. She's our local historian and expert storyteller. Are you a journalist?"

Wren smiled and nodded. "I'm Wren Weaver, and this is Rascal."

The librarian nodded. "Related to the Williams family in Georgia on your mother's side; we're glad to have you here, Wren. I'm Lilibeth. Our writers' group would love to have you speak to them. Will you be here in three weeks? That's their next meeting."

"I'm really sorry that I won't be here; I'm on a tight schedule and will have to leave for my next assignment in about a week."

"One of our patrons runs a podcast on Saturdays at ten thirty. If I give you a list of questions from the writers' group by lunchtime today, do you think you could address some of them on the podcast?"

"I've never done anything like that." Wren felt her pulse quicken. "I'm afraid I might freeze up."

"Could you read a brief excerpt from an article you've written? Maybe five or ten minutes? The listeners would love it."

"I could find something; that would make it a lot easier for me than fielding questions," Wren said.

"Good, then plan on being here at ten in the morning. I'll give you a list of questions before you leave, and you can pick two or three for the podcaster to ask you to fill the rest of the twenty minutes." The woman rose from her seat and came out from behind the desk.

"Come with me, and I'll introduce you to our resident storyteller, Miss Ruth Whitaker. We have a small conference room where the two of you can have some privacy."

Lilibeth stopped at a table where a lone elderly woman wore a headset; the woman smiled and nodded as she listened, and her clear blue eyes stared blankly ahead.

The librarian lightly tapped on the table, and the woman removed her headset.

"Miss Ruth, our visiting journalist from Georgia is here. Wren's assignment is to write articles about haunted campgrounds. Could you fill her in on Bootleggers Creek?"

Ruth smiled. "I could do that; tell me what she looks like."

"She has sparkling green eyes with undertones of blue; her skin is pale, and her curly hair is light brown with dominate streaks of natural, wild red. She has a hiking staff because she twisted her ankle. Even though she's young and petite, you'll probably sense a toughness about her because I did. She has her companion, Rascal, with her; he's a handsome black and tan Labrador retriever with a beautiful, curved tail like a Husky."

"Natural red hair, Lilibeth?" Ruth asked.

"Strong streaks of natural red hair that refuse to blend in," Lilibeth said.

Ruth put her hand down, and Rascal gently nudged it. She tittered. "What a sweet boy."

"I thought y'all could chat in the conference room."

After Ruth rose from her seat, Lilibeth stood next to her.

"On your left, Miss Ruth."

Wren and Rascal followed the two women to a short hallway and into a small room with a round table and four chairs.

After the librarian guided Ruth to a chair, Wren asked, "Miss Ruth, I have my laptop with me; do you mind if I jot down a word or two once in a while?"

"Whatever is easy for you, dear," Ruth said.

"I'm not a transcriptionist, so you don't have to feel you're dictating your story."

Ruth smiled. "That's good to know; if you did, I'd swear you made it up."

Wren giggled. "I do love a good story, but my articles are all completely based on facts and legends."

"Facts and legends?" Lilibeth smiled. "Literary license at its best."

After the librarian quietly closed the door as she left, Ruth said, "Tell me a little about your assignment and the magazine."

Wren said, "The magazine is a travel magazine; my assignment is to write articles about four campgrounds across the United States that are reported to be haunted. Bootleggers Creek is my third campground; the other two were in Arizona and Texas. I love camping, so the assignment was perfect for me. When I registered at Bootleggers Creek, my folder included a history of the campground."

"What did you think about it?"

"It was very generic with no details or even a hint that the campground is haunted. It said that Bootleggers Creek was the site of a bootlegger's still from the 1920s until the 1950s when the bootlegger walked away from his lucrative operation after his grandson died in a crash on a mountain road while he was taking a heavy load of moonshine to a wealthy customer."

Ruth snorted. "You're right about generic; I'd call it whitewashed. I have some facts that may fill in a few holes. The original bootlegger in the 1920s was a man named Clarence Whitaker; he had the right equipment and the skills to make his famous, high quality, smooth whiskey."

"Really?" Wren asked. "Sorry for the interruption."

"Yes, he was my great-grandfather. My dad was the oldest of his grandsons. The grandson who died in the crash was George, but they called him 'Ghost Driver' because he named his blue car Blue Ghost when he first started driving. Over time, the stories about his speed and his ability to elude any pursuers supported the legend of Ghost Driver, and his name was shortened to 'Ghost.' I barely remember him, but Mom told me I called him Uncle Ghost, and it tickled him. My dad told me that his youngest brother started driving moonshine when he was eleven years old, and my dad, who was in high school, had to go with him, so no one would try to take advantage of a young boy.

Ghost couldn't read or write, but he was a genius with numbers and a talented car mechanic. Dad said that by the time Ghost was twelve, he had a reputation for delivering on time and not taking any guff, and none of the buyers crossed him."

"Wow; imagine commanding that much respect at twelve years of age."

Ruth nodded. "Dad said at first Ghost's driving scared him because he drove so fast, but Dad quickly appreciated his brother's skills."

"So, how was it possible that Ghost crashed?"

"It wasn't, unless he was murdered. Only Uncle Ghost and his murderer know the truth."

Wren furrowed her brow. "Why did Clarence Whitaker walk away?"

"He didn't; I don't have any facts, but the family lore is that his rivals caught him alone at his still, murdered him, and stole his equipment. My dad told me that wasn't true because his grandfather had given away his equipment to a friend, but Dad never said who that was, and I was always afraid to question Dad."

"So, why is Bootleggers Creek haunted?"

"Nobody knows, but I think Uncle Ghost is waiting for his opportunity for a rematch with his killer."

"But wouldn't his killer be dead by now?"

"The family has always believed in blood revenge. You haven't typed anything, Wren."

Wren chuckled. "No, I haven't, but I do have another question: who was Clarence Whitaker's major rival?"

"Now, why do you ask? No one else has ever asked me that before, and I must have told this story at least a hundred times."

"It's logical; who?"

Ruth fanned her face with her hand and exhaled. "I'm plumb wore out; maybe we can talk another time when I'm feeling stronger."

Wren crossed her arms and remained silent. *Don't go pulling a Miss Jenna Lee on me.*

"Didn't you hear what I said, girl? I'm an old woman, and I'm tired."

Wren rolled her eyes and waited.

Ruth slammed her fist on the table. "Why haven't you answered me?"

"I was being polite and waiting for you to answer me first." Wren bit her lip. *I'm harassing an old, blind woman.*

"You're harassing an old, blind woman," Ruth hissed.

Wren's eyes widened. "I was just thinking the very same thing. How did you know that?"

Ruth burst out laughing. "It's logical."

Wren giggled. "We certainly share an unusual sense of humor."

"We surely do; I knew you musta had eighty proof Whitaker blood in you by your hair that won't let that watered-down Williams hair have a seat at the table. Clarence Whitaker's major rival was a no-good snake, Norman Hudson. Fifteen years after Clarence Whitaker became established as a quality moonshiner, Norman Hudson jumped into the business, but he cut corners; his 'shine wasn't smooth and smelled like bad breath. My dad said Norman Hudson was ate up by jealousy because he couldn't match a third of Clarence Whitaker's sales even after he tried to undercut him with slashed prices. Norman Hudson's family had a falling out that caused a chasm between the brothers right after Clarence Whitaker died; two of the brothers kept up Norman Hudson's questionable business practices and their business finally failed not long after their dad died, but the third, who was a good friend of Dad's, went a different direction. That's all I have for you."

We're done. Wren rose from her seat. "Thank you for everything, Miss Ruth. I enjoyed our chat and appreciate the time you set aside for me."

"Thank you, Wren. You hear his engine, don't you?"

Ah ha. This is why she agreed to talk to me. Wren stopped before she opened the door. "If the engine is Ghost's, then yes, I hear it."

Ruth snorted. "I don't know who else's it could be. Do those people who run the campground live on site?"

"I don't think so."

"Be interesting to find out why not."

"Thanks. You know, I don't even know their name."

Ruth sneered, "It's Hudson."

Wow.

Wren held onto her hiking stick for assistance as she walked to the desk; Rascal trotted ahead and waited for her along with Lilibeth.

"We had a wonderful visit with Miss Ruth; thank you so much for arranging it," Wren said.

"You're quite welcome; it must really have been something because Miss Ruth has never had a meeting with anyone that lasted longer than ten minutes." The librarian beamed. "Here are your questions; I'll see you in the morning at ten."

"I do have a question for you. Why are pets allowed in the library?"

"They're housebroken, know how to behave, and never turn in a book late."

The librarian glanced around then lowered her voice, "I can't say that about most of our two-legged patrons."

Rascal grinned, and the librarian slipped him a treat. "Thank you, Rascal; very few of those misbehaving human creatures think I'm funny; their loss because they never get any treats."

Chapter Four

Before Wren left the library parking lot, she said, "This has been a very productive morning. Let's stop at the grocery store to find something for supper."

After she parked at the grocery store, Wren checked the weather. "Today won't be as warm as yesterday, and we may have rain this afternoon."

She sent Justin a text. "Productive morning at the library. We can talk later."

He responded. "Good news. I love hearing from my honey. Ly."

Wren sighed as she texted, "Miss you. Ly 2."

She opened her door. "I won't be long, Rascal."

While Wren examined the meals in the refrigerated case, two women behind her chatted.

"Did you hear what happened at the campground? A man wandered off in the rain last night on foot. They just found his body three miles away from the campground in a ravine. I heard he was drunk."

"No, really? Three miles is a long way to have walked at night, much less in the middle of that rainstorm we had. I couldn't even see past the front porch. How'd they find him? Those ravines are steep."

"I didn't catch that part. How much rain did you get? Our rain gauge had over two inches, and our driveway was still flooded early this morning. I told that worthless husband of mine that we shouldn't buy a house in the valley, but Mr. Big Shot never listens to me."

The women continued to talk about the rain and husbands as they walked away.

Wren picked out another chicken meal in a sack then went to the produce section to look for fruit to have on hand. While she inspected the apples, a young woman with a toddler in her shopping cart stopped next to her.

"If you're interested in apples, you may want to go to Jack's Apple Orchard." She chuckled. "My husband works there, so I might be a bit prejudiced, but their apples are worth the trip, and their apple butter is to die for."

Wren smiled. "Thanks; that's a great idea."

"It's a pleasant drive; you'll enjoy it."

The toddler grinned as he waved goodbye at Wren when his mother turned to the next aisle; Wren smiled and returned his wave.

After she was in her pickup, she looked up the address for Jack's Apple Orchard on her phone.

"Ready for a road trip, Rascal? We can drop off the groceries at the camper then go to Jack's Apple Orchard, where Dana Grace works. It sounds like a good place to get apples."

While Wren put her meal in the small refrigerator inside the camper, her phone rang.

"Hi, Betsy. How are you doing?"

"Awful. The school board picked that candidate who has been pestering Justin over the young male teacher from Phoenix. I'm irritated mostly because the young man and Natalie at the diner really hit it off. My friends and I were planning a surprise engagement party for them and everything."

"Who's Natalie?" Wren asked.

"The best server we've ever had at the Watering Hole; are you forgetting about us already?"

"I don't think I knew her name."

"Are you sure? Maybe you've just forgotten because everybody knows Natalie."

"I don't remember hearing her name, and I'm not sure I'd know her outside of the watering hole because she was a blur."

Betsy chuckled. "She does move fast, doesn't she? Well, she certainly caught the eye of our young male teacher from Phoenix who grew up in Tombstone. We think she gave him her number. One of my friends thought she saw Natalie stop a second and answer a text right after she dropped off an order."

"I can't imagine Natalie stopping. So, what are you going to do about the candidate the school board selected?"

"My friend who is on the town council is going to talk to the chairperson of the school board and remind them that they'll be replacing the teacher before next year. She'll remind them that the teacher was particularly interested in Justin, and she'll leave Hidden Gulch with a broken heart. We don't think the board thought about how mean that would be of them."

Wren smiled. *That's one way.*

"Just in case that doesn't work," Betsy said, "we're inviting the teacher to your um...surprise party to welcome you back."

She's not telling me something.

"Really?"

"Yes, I'd like to take credit for it, but it was Socorro's idea; you're not supposed to know about it because it's a surprise, so you can't say anything to anybody, especially Justin because we haven't told him yet. Socorro thinks he might tell you, so we're keeping it low key until we know the date you'll be back."

Wren sighed. "I suppose I'll get the details later about this surprise party that no one knows about that will be held on a date to be determined, and when the selected teacher candidate hears about it, she'll decline the position."

"Exactly; I'm glad you approve. Are you doing okay? What are you and Rascal doing today?"

"We're going to an apple orchard; I understand they have great apple butter."

"That sounds like fun; I'll talk to you later. I'm supposed to call the teacher we don't want here."

After Betsy hung up, Wren frowned. "Betsy and her friends are definitely in a conspiracy; what bothers me is that I'm somehow involved too."

"Ready for a short walk? Let's go to the registration office to see if the owner is more congenial this morning."

On the way, Wren frowned at the site where the Texas State man's RV had been. *His RV is gone.*

When they entered the registration office, an elderly woman smiled as she stocked ice cream into the chest freezer. "Good morning, you must be Wren; I'm Lorinda Cooper. My daughter and her husband manage my campground for me. I'm filling in, so they could go to Chattanooga; they'll return late Sunday. Who's your companion?"

"This is Rascal."

"You're a handsome boy, Rascal. How did you sleep with all that rain, Wren?"

Wren smiled. "It was definitely noisy."

Lorinda slid the freezer's glass top closed. "What can I do for you?"

"I'm a journalist; my publisher sent me here because I'm writing articles about haunted campgrounds. I read the history of the campground, but there wasn't any mention of it being haunted, so I thought I'd check to see if there was more to its story."

"You have certainly found a hornets' nest to poke at with that writer's pen. I've lived here for over fifty years, and even though my family comes from here, I'm considered a newcomer because I was born in Memphis. My daughter, Estelle, was born here, so she claims she's a local and calls me a newcomer. Biggest mistake I ever made was not to drive myself to Chattanooga to have that snooty child." Lorinda chuckled.

"When did you buy the campground?"

"My husband and I bought it from my son-in-law's family twenty years ago because the bank was about to foreclose on them. At the time, we thought it was a good idea to keep it locally owned and to give our Estelle and her husband, Chester, income by managing it. I'm not sure how well suited they are for managing a campground because of their lack of people skills, but they do a good job of keeping it up."

"They certainly do; this is one of the best maintained campgrounds I've seen."

"Looks aren't everything though, are they? The locals don't admit to any skeletons in their closets, which is why that so-called history is so watered-down. I wrote the original history, but my daughter edited it. I don't know why she even bothered to pretend to use mine; when I asked her, she told me it was because I was the boss because that's what her husband calls me. Do you have an email address? I'll send you the original, but you can't tell anyone how you got the information; give credit to the tree fairies, which is what I call the lightning bugs because it irritates my daughter or maybe don't mention the tree fairies because she would know it came from me." Lorinda tittered as she pointed to the notepad on the desk.

"That would be great." Wren wrote her email address on Lorinda's pad.

"Tell me more about your assignment," Lorinda said.

"This is my third campground. My first article is published, and my second article is in the process of being published."

"That's exciting; is there a way I can read your first article?"

Wren wrote the magazine's website on the notepad. "My publisher owns a travel magazine. There's a sample of the article on the website; you can subscribe if you'd like to read the rest of the campground article and the magazine."

"A travel magazine? That could be dangerous; I might find some places I'd like to visit."

Wren smiled. "I think that's what my publisher lives for."

"I'll get my history to you before the end of the day. It hasn't been edited, so please don't judge me for my poor editing skills."

"That's not my job; just ask my editor," Wren smiled.

"You have a publisher and an editor? I'm really jealous."

"My editor is a jerk and thinks I'm incompetent; the publisher spends all his time trying to appease both of us, which usually ends in me threatening to quit. I'm jealous of writers with skilled editors."

Lorinda laughed. "Okay, maybe I'm only partly jealous then. How long are you going to be here?"

"My tentative plan is to have my article written by Monday, but no later than Tuesday, then I'll have my own editor review it before I send it to the publisher."

"Let me know how I can help."

"Thank you. I might have some questions for clarification after I read your history of the campground."

"I noticed you're using a hiking staff; are you okay?"

"I twisted my ankle, but it's much better. I'm being extra cautious, so I don't reinjure it."

"Have you walked the trail behind the campground? It's a comfortable walk and goes around the pond that is fed by Bootleggers Creek and is a little more than a mile long. Go past the last row, then instead of turning toward the bathrooms, go the other way. I can't remember if it's on the campground map, but it's level and well-maintained, which probably is not a surprise to you, and it's a lovely walk through the woods that I'm sure you and Rascal will enjoy. You might want to take an umbrella because the tree leaves are still very wet from that rain;

when the wind blows, you'll think it's raining because of the light shower on the trail under the tall trees."

After Wren and Rascal left the office, Wren said, "Today has the potential of becoming a productive day after all, doesn't it, Rascal? The trail sounds good to me. I'll wear my rain jacket and hat, then we'll look for the trail."

Wren pulled out her rain gear backpack from her pickup; after she put on her rain jacket and hat, they headed to the last row of campsites.

Rascal bounded ahead then returned to Wren and led her to the trail. "I'm glad I put on my jacket, Rascal; it's cooler in the shade of the woods."

As she strolled along the trail, Wren listened to a mockingbird that ran through its repertoire and to the whistles of a hawk. Two crows called to each other.

"I'll bet those are the crows assigned to keep track of the hawk," Wren said.

When she came to a bench alongside the trail, Wren sat down. A slight breeze rustled the leaves in the treetops, and Wren laughed at the sudden shower.

After they continued on the path, Wren peered through the trees at the pond then stopped to watch the fish jump for the water bugs on the surface.

When they were halfway around the trail, Wren glanced to her left. "There's a cleared area there, Rascal. Let's check it out."

After they made their way through the woods to the clearing, they were at the edge of an enormous field with a dirt track that circled the perimeter of the field.

A slight young man stood in the middle of the field with his arms crossed. He wore a brown, flat cap over his shock of red hair and a brown shirt; brown suspenders held up his brown houndstooth print britches. The laces on his scuffed work boots were frayed.

"What are you doing here, doll?"

Wren stared; when the young man turned to leave, she asked, "Are you George?"

He turned back and glowered at her with fire in his clear blue eyes. "I only heard that name one time, and that was at the gol-dang funeral."

"Sorry, Ghost; I was just a little startled for a minute there."

He narrowed his eyes. "Hold on. How come you can see and hear me?"

Ghost disappeared.

Wren blinked. "Did you see him, Rascal?"

Rascal yipped.

Wren stared at the field for another five minutes but didn't see or hear anything until a hawk swooped into the field and grabbed a field mouse then flew away with the two crows following him.

Wren exhaled. "I guess we'll continue our walk."

Before she reached the end of the trail where it came out at the campground, Wren said, "I'm eager to read Lorinda's version of the history of the campground. We'll go to Jack's Apple Orchard Gift Shop after lunch; it will be nice to have a diversion while we wait for the email from Lorinda."

After they were in the camper, Wren made herself half of a sandwich while Rascal drank his fill of water.

While she ate her sandwich, she added a few more paragraphs to "High Falutin' Killers".

"I'll be sad when the story ends because I'm enjoying the characters. Maybe I'll pick another one of Miranda's stories and write book two with the same characters. I don't think Miranda would mind. I'm sorry I had to put the box on the floor in the backseat, but I kept tripping over it in this tiny camper; it doesn't crowd you, does it?"

Rascal sat for his after-lunch treat; Wren chuckled. "Okay, here's your reward."

After she put the knife and her plate in her dishpan, Wren said, "Maybe we should wash dishes before we leave. Do you want to go with me to the laundry room, or do you want some time to relax?"

Rascal flopped down on the floor and closed his eyes.

Wren carried the dishpan on her hip with one hand, so she could steady herself with her hiking stick.

After she quickly washed then rinsed her dishes, she returned to the camper and checked the weather.

"There's a little higher chance of rain in the next hour, Rascal. I'm a little nervous about driving in the rain, but I don't think I'll be able to hide from rain on the road for the next three weeks."

She exhaled. "Let's go; it's only twenty-five minutes from here. If the clouds start gathering, we'll head back. We won't be there all that long anyway because we don't want to monopolize Dana Grace's time. How long can it take to buy a couple of apples and some apple butter? Ten minutes, max, right?"

On the way to the gift shop, Wren said, "I want to look over the questions from Lilibeth after we return; I was kind of avoiding them. Now I wished I'd said I was busy, but she was right when she said it would be a good experience for me."

After Wren turned at the large Jack's Apple Orchard Gift Shop sign, she was surprised at the number of cars in the parking lot. "That little store must be packed. Let's just turn around and go back."

Rascal growled.

"I'll park then peek inside the door; if it's too crowded, we'll come back another time. I should have realized Friday would be a busy day."

Rascal waited on the porch while Wren opened the gift shop door. Her eyes widened. *There's no one here.*

Dana Grace smiled. "Hi, Wren. You just missed the orchard tour. We had a huge crowd, but the bus is large, so everyone got a seat. What brings you this way?"

"Apples and apple butter," Wren said.

"We have an array of apple butters." Dana Grace motioned toward the back wall. "Pick out a few, and I'll give you the lowdown on each one. You want eating apples, I assume. How many?"

"How about four?" Wren strolled to the shelves with apple butter.

"Your hiking staff is beautiful. Is it new?"

"Thank you. I bought it at the camping store in Dearheart; I twisted my ankle and needed something sturdy, so my ankle could heal."

When Dana Grace returned from the back room with a small, brown paper sack of apples, Wren carried two jars of apple butter to the register.

"These two; are there any others you'd suggest?"

"I have two more with similar apples that I'm sure you'll like."

"Is Jack your uncle?" Wren asked while Dana Grace brought two more jars to the register.

Dana Grace giggled. "No, Jack's Apple Orchard is a play on words. Have you ever heard of applejack? It's essentially Tennessee Apple Brandy. The original Hudson who started the orchard in the 1950s was Andrew Jackson Hudson. Jack's Apple Orchard was his way of thumbing his nose at the ATF because in addition to apples and apple butter, A.J., as everyone called him, distilled the best applejack in the mountains. The recipe and the equipment have been passed down through the years in the family. Uncle Samuel is almost embarrassed to admit that he has a license to make and sell hard cider and applejack. The orchard tour guides imply that both the hard cider and applejack are illegal, and the tourists eat it up; people love being a little bit shady, don't they? Did you see the applejack butter? It's labeled A.J. butter, and it's our biggest seller."

"A.J. butter? Applejack from A.J. right under the revenuers' noses." Wren giggled. "I'll need four jars of A.J. butter too; they'll be perfect gifts for Mom and a couple of my friends."

Dana Grace said, "We have a second section that we call Crafty Artisans. We feature items from local crafters on consignment; you might see something else for gifts. The original still is on display in there."

"The original still? Did A.J. make the still himself?"

Dana Grace smiled. "The family legend is that an old friend gave him the still to keep it from being destroyed; the family has assumed the old friend learned the revenuers planned to raid his still, and A.J.'s respectable apple orchard was the perfect place to hide it."

When they went into the Crafty Artisans room, Wren's eyes widened at the large copper container with its copper coils that was contained inside a tall glass display case. The old still had transformed from gleaming orange to a soft green patina over the years.

Wren walked around the case to examine the still. "Wow, the still is a really impressive piece of art in its own right, isn't it?"

"I think so; visitors often ask why we don't scrub the green away. As part of our tour, we include a short video that explains the chemical reaction of copper by using the example of the Statue of Liberty that was the traditional brilliant orange copper color when it arrived in the United States. We explain that if the green is scrubbed away, the copper will begin its slow chemical reaction from orange to brown to green."

Wren stared at the still. "Here's a dark brown spot; is that why the still is in the glass case?"

"You have an eagle eye for detail; when I was four or five, Uncle Samuel caught a persistent visitor scrubbing the still with steel wool. She claimed he threatened to cook her in the pot; everyone laughed at her because my uncle is such a kind-hearted man, except he's extra particular when it comes to the orchard business. Mom told me years later that's exactly what Uncle

Samuel said, and she was going to help him, but the visitor ran to her car."

Wren giggled. "I love it; that is the best example of poetic justice I've ever heard."

Wren frowned at the sound of a low rumble. "Rascal and I need to head back to the campground; thank you for stories."

Chapter Five

On the way to the cash register, Dana Grace said, "I read the sample of your article about the Arizona campground. I subscribed to the magazine, so I could read the rest. I love your style of writing. When do you expect the next article to be published?"

"No telling; it will be in the next magazine, but the publisher doesn't seem to have a rigorous schedule, which drives me crazy."

Dana Grace nodded as she rang up Wren's purchases. "That must be maddening for a journalist; aren't you normally driven by deadlines?"

Wren paid for her items. "Always; I've never worked with such a loose schedule, so I set my own deadlines."

"I'll put your items in a box then carry it out for you."

After Dana Grace set the box on the floor of the back seat, she scanned the sky. "You've got plenty of time to get back to the campground before it rains, but I'll bet it's going to be a gully washer again. Hear the cicadas buzz? If it's storming when I get off work, I'll go home with my uncle and aunt."

On the way back to the campground, Wren said, "That was a profitable trip in more ways than one. As soon as we return to the campground, I'd like to take a shower if I can before it rains."

After she parked in front of her camper, Wren went inside and grabbed her shower bag and her towel. On the way to the shower, she said, "I won't be long."

She shampooed her hair then washed with shower soap and her loofah that she called her scrubbie. As she dried herself, a loud crack of thunder shook the frosted window, and the lights flickered.

Wren threw on her clothes then realized she had to wear her boots back to the camper. She put on her dirty socks and her boots before she grabbed up her shower gear.

"I didn't think this through; I forgot my staff and flip flops." She forced herself to watch her steps as she hurried to her site as fast as she dared.

After they reached the camper, Rascal scrambled inside; Wren jumped when a nearby streak of lightning was followed by a loud crash of thunder.

"I'm turning into a real scaredy-cat when it comes to thunderstorms, Rascal."

She poured herself a glass of tea then pulled out the questions from Lilibeth.

After she read the questions, she frowned. "Lilibeth said this will be the closing question, Rascal. 'How can our listeners support you and your work?' It would be really lame for me to tell the listeners to subscribe to a magazine that will probably have only four of my articles. I need a website. I think I just gave myself a project that's going to take me all night unless I can pull off something smart. Who could advise me on how to create a web page?"

While she drank her tea, heavy rain suddenly hit the camper. "Gage, who was the co-owner of our last campground, the Lonesome Trail in Texas, was also a marketing guy; he would know who could help me."

Wren sent Gage a text. "I need a website by tomorrow morning. Can you give me any advice?"

Her phone rang.

"Thanks for calling, Gage, but it's really not an emergency."

"If you need a website by tomorrow morning and don't know how to create one, it is. Tell me why you need a website and what you want on it."

"I'm going to be on a local podcast tomorrow morning at ten o'clock; I've never done a podcast before, but they gave me a list of questions, and the last one is how can listeners support you and your work?"

"You're smart to think of a web page. What do you want on it?"

"I don't know; it would be nice to have a blog."

"That's perfect; why don't we have a simple landing page and your blog. What are you going to blog?"

"I'd like to blog stories."

"What kind of stories? Fiction, under 1,500 words, like flash fiction?"

"I'd like that; it will help me develop my fiction writing skills; I'm working on a novel."

"You can also blog about your trials with writing a novel to make your blog a little more interesting. What do you want to call your blog?"

Wren exhaled. "I have no idea at all."

"What about Short and Swift Stories, or Briefly Told? Your website could be Wrens Journal, Wrens Rag, Wrens Chronicles, Wrens Twist, or something like that depending on the availability of the website. We can't use an apostrophe; is that okay with you? I need a photo of you; do you have a selfie, or better yet, one of you and Rascal?"

"I can text one to you."

"Give me about an hour; I'll call you back with a test website to see what you think. It will be super simple, but it will give you something to tell the listeners tomorrow."

"You don't have to do this, Gage. I didn't mean..."

"This is what I love: being creative under a killer deadline with no prisoners taken." Gage chuckled as he hung up.

Wren texted him the photo of her and Rascal together.

Gage replied, "Got it."

"I didn't expect that, Rascal. Gage is going to set up a web page for me, so I'll have a blog tomorrow morning. I guess I need to write something, so my blog will have something in it. He had a bunch of suggestions for the webpage and the blog; I like Wrens Twist for the website and Briefly Told for the blog the best. I'll send him a text."

After she sent the text to Gage, he immediately replied, "Good choices. On it."

Wren exhaled. "I think I can rework the first chapter of 'High Falutin' Killers' into a flash fiction story, but I'll call it something else."

Wren read her first chapter. "Actually, I can write a prequel as a flash fiction story."

Wren typed furiously for over an hour until her phone buzzed a text then rang.

"Ready to see your website, Wren?" Gage asked. "I sent you the link, but I sent it to Mom first; she loved it, so you have your first fan."

"That's awesome." Wren typed in the link on her computer.

"Wow, this is beautiful, Gage. I love the colors."

"Mom said your website captured the color of your eyes. The website includes an About the Author page you can revise whenever you feel like it, and the Contact Me goes to your email. I set up an email for Wren at Wrens Twist dot com, but that probably won't be live before tomorrow morning. I'll email you the instructions on how to add and update your blog, then maybe we can spend a little time tomorrow after your podcast talking about your website and beefing it up a bit more. Let Mom and me know when you have your blog finished. Mom wants to read it before tomorrow. I think you have a ready-made blog editor. I have a couple of tweaks I'd like to do before tomorrow, but I don't want to be shifting things around while you're blogging. Oh, Tara said to tell you hi and thanks for giving me a project; she's agreed to be our accountant and is here setting up our accounting and claims I hover too much."

"That is wonderful news; tell her hello from me."

"Tara thought of something else. Send us the link to the podcast, so we can listen in. Talk to you later."

Wren smiled after she hung up. "I think Tara has forgiven Gage after all, Rascal. I'm really glad."

Wren sent Lilibeth an email asking for the link to the podcast; Lilibeth replied with the link almost immediately.

Wren read over the instructions that Gage sent her. "I think I can do this."

Wren copied then pasted her story into the blog. After she read it, she said, "I think it's fine; I'll probably want to rewrite it after I've written more stories and my skills improve, but it's not terrible." Wren snickered. "I almost feel like calling it 'The Story That Isn't Awful.'"

She sent Gage a text: "Blog's done. This is the link to the podcast at ten o'clock, Tennessee time."

Her phone buzzed a text; she smiled. *Justin.*

"How's your day?"

"I was invited to be interviewed on a podcast tomorrow morning. I've never done one before. We can talk later."

"You'll be great. Ly."

Wren responded, "Ly 2."

Wren exhaled then glanced outside. "I'm not very original, am I, Rascal? The rain has stopped; how about a walk before supper?"

Wren put on her rain hat and rain jacket then picked up her staff. When they went outside, Wren took off her jacket and hat and tossed them into the camper.

"It's a lot warmer than I expected, and the humidity is awful. This feels like Georgia, doesn't it, Rascal?"

Rascal yipped.

As they walked toward the registration office, Wren said, "I still need the story of the haunted campground before I can submit my article. I'm hoping Lorinda will have something for me."

The office was closed, so they headed toward the restrooms and continued, but instead of taking the trail that led to where they saw Ghost, Rascal went the other way to a path that Wren hadn't noticed earlier. The path had been cleared recently and was wide enough for two people to walk comfortably next to each other but wasn't groomed like the trail had been.

Wren followed Rascal deeper into the woods; the path narrowed to accommodate only single file foot travel. The path seemed to stop, but Rascal continued and led Wren through the brush between the trees.

When Rascal stopped, Wren shivered as the temperature suddenly dropped and peered ahead at the old clapboard house with a wide, wraparound porch and a tin roof.

"Whose house is that?" she asked.

"Grandpap's house." Ghost stood next to Wren. "You shouldn't be here, doll. Grandpap's not here no more, and these people are trouble. Now, git." Ghost disappeared.

Wren shuddered as an icy chill ran down her spine and the hair on the back of her neck rose. "Let's go, Rascal."

Rascal led the way through the brush and back to the path. When they returned to the camper, Wren poured herself another glass of sweet tea then fed Rascal.

"How do I find out who lives there? Do you think Lorinda might know? I think that was still campground property because we didn't go past any fences or even fence posts, but that's just a guess on my part. I can't just ask her, though, because I was probably trespassing."

Wren pulled out her sack from the grocery store with her dinner and peered inside. "I should have read the instructions; this is a meal for two and takes a little more prep, but I'll be okay because I'll have leftovers for tomorrow."

The two chicken thighs were already rubbed with spices, so Wren put them into her air fryer before she pulled out the premade salad and dressing then carried the rest of the ingredients to her outdoor kitchen.

"I need to boil water for the fettucine noodles." She exhaled. "This is really inconvenient; I'll take the pot to the laundry and pour out the water after I eat."

While she waited for the water to boil, Wren put the onion and garlic in the pan along with some olive oil and heated them until they were soft then stirred the noodles into the boiling water. She mixed the rest of the chopped ingredients with the onion and garlic in the pan and gave the vegetables a quick stir.

"Now I'm supposed to add the chicken thighs," she grumbled.

Wren turned off the burner under the vegetables and went inside for the chicken.

"I have ten more minutes to wait for the chicken, Rascal. The fettucine will be done by then. Why did the instructions tell me to start the noodles so early?"

Wren's phone buzzed a text from Gage's mother, Kendra.

"Love your website; love your blog! Will listen to the podcast tomorrow."

Wren replied, "Thank you."

She smiled. *I'll send the link to Justin and Betsy; they'll be excited for me too.*

She texted messages first to Justin then to Betsy with the link to her new website.

The bell dinged on the air fryer; Wren removed the chicken and carried it outside. After she diced the chicken, she added it to the vegetables and stirred in the rest of the spices.

When the fettucine was ready, she dipped it into the pan with the meat and vegetables then stirred everything together before she turned off her burner and went into the camper with the pan. She dished up a serving into a bowl and sat at her small table with the salad and her chicken supper. She stared at her glass of sweet tea that was on the counter next to the air fryer then sighed. "I'll get it in a minute; I'm hungry."

After she took her first bite, Wren said, "This is actually good, or else I'm starving from running back and forth while I did all the prep."

While she ate, her phone rang; she smiled as she answered Justin's call. "I hope I didn't pull you out of one of your..."

Justin interrupted. "How long have you been working on that website? You haven't said a word about it."

"I didn't..."

He broke in again. "Did you pay somebody? I showed it to Terry, and she said it was a professional website and was very expensive. Why didn't you let me know? They probably charged you way too much. Why haven't you said anything? I know people who could have done it for much less."

Wren pulled away the phone from her face and pursed her lips to keep from screaming at him. She straightened her back and cleared her throat before she spoke in an icy voice and carefully enunciated each word. "You showed it to whom?"

"It doesn't matter; you..."

Wren cut him off. "I'm in the middle of eating my supper; if you don't have anything else, I'll call you after I eat."

She hung up and stabbed her salad with her fork.

"Maybe I'll call after I finish eating breakfast," she fumed. "On Monday."

Betsy sent her a text. "Your website is gorgeous, Wren."

Before Wren could reply to the text, her phone rang. She glared at her phone then smiled. *It's Betsy; I can answer it.*

"Wren, I loved your blog and subscribed to it, so I'll be notified by email the next time you post; how often are you planning to blog?" Betsy asked.

I didn't know the blog had been set up for readers to subscribe. Gage is a genius.

"I hadn't thought that far ahead; what do you think?"

"I'd love to read your blog every day, but that would take away from your novel that you're writing and your actual life. A lot of bloggers post weekly, but because you're posting a complete story, once a month would be perfect, or you could post twice a month: a story at the first of the month, then maybe a short piece in the middle of the month about your work, like where you are in your novel, a bit about your main character or the bad guy, or challenges in writing. Consistency is definitely the key, so your readers know what to expect."

"That's brilliant advice; you sound like an expert. Do you follow other bloggers?"

Betsy giggled. "Does it show? A few; I love reading blogs."

"I should have known."

Wren inhaled then exhaled quietly to maintain a casual tone in her voice. "Any resolution on the teacher situation?"

"Not so far, but Terry and I are having coffee tomorrow morning. She's here for the weekend to find a place to live."

"That might be hard."

"You're right; Terry said there aren't any houses or even any apartments available for rent in her price range, and she doesn't have a camper or anything, so she can't stay at the campground. She mentioned she would like to find someone with a spare bedroom that wouldn't mind having a roommate. Terry asked me if I had a spare bedroom, and I told her no; she said she'd keep asking around." Betsy chuckled. "Butch and I aren't the roommate types."

After they hung up, Wren growled, "I knew it, Rascal."

She dumped the rest of her meal into the trash. "My appetite is completely ruined. I'm glad I wrote my blog before Justin called."

She plugged in her phone to charge and tapped the 'Do Not Disturb' setting.

She opened her laptop. "Lorinda sent me the history she wrote. Maybe I'll become immersed in the campground's history and forget about Justin and his Terry."

She checked her website one more time before she opened the email. "It's absolutely perfect. I wonder what Gage is tweaking? I'll bet it's behind the scenes stuff."

She smiled at Lorinda's email. "I wrote this quite a while ago; it's pretty rough because it's never been edited. The first few pages are back story that I didn't include in the history, but I thought you might like to read. I'll be at the registration office tomorrow at eight if you have any questions, or if you feel like dropping by and telling me it isn't as awful as I think it is."

Wren opened the document and raised her eyebrows. "This is much longer than I expected."

When she finished reading the first three pages, she said, "Rascal, Lorinda's back story is from the perspective of her family. Her great-grandfather was the sheriff when Clarence Whitaker and Norman Hudson were bootleggers. Sheriff Cooper had a great deal of respect for Clarence Whitaker because he cared about his customers, but the sheriff didn't care much at all for Norman Hudson because he'd caused several deaths with toxic batches of moonshine. According to Lorinda, Sheriff Cooper was obsessed with arresting Norman Hudson for murder; it was a frequent topic at the dinner table in the Cooper home. She mentioned that Sheriff Cooper was convinced the two Hudson sons who took over the Whitaker property were behind Ghost's death, and probably Clarence Whitaker's too, but he was frustrated because he didn't have any evidence. Lorinda said the Whitaker property included the homestead, the still, and a dirt stock car raceway in addition to the primitive campground with a few sites and an outhouse. The third Hudson son was A.J. Hudson who bought land and started an apple orchard. Lorinda makes it clear that her husband is related to A.J. Hudson, and her son-in-law is related to the Hudsons who took over the campground."

Wren smiled. "Lorinda doesn't have a very high opinion of her son-in-law and his family; she tried to convince Estelle that she shouldn't marry Chester Hudson because they were cousins, but Estelle ignored her; probably because they're like fourth or fifth cousins."

After Wren read the next two pages, she said, "Everything that was on the campground history sheet came from Lorinda's document. I don't understand why Estelle didn't leave the history of the stock car raceway in it because it's really interesting. It was a big draw on Friday and Saturday nights for entertainment, and at one time the raceway had a concession stand and bleachers around the track for the fans who parked at a parking lot that wasn't far from the campground. Stock car races became less popular over the decades as the drivers and mechanics became older and retired; the younger generation didn't have the thrill of driving bootleg whiskey during the week then racing their cars on Friday nights at the raceway. The legend is that the old-timers still get together from time to time to race their ghostly cars on the raceway, and you can hear the sound of the crowds cheering and the racing engines from the campground."

Wren stared at the last page. *I have everything I need for my article, but I wonder where the old parking lot is.*

Wren replied to Lorinda's email. "I loved it; I'll see you in the morning and gush appropriately."

Lorinda replied immediately, "Thank you, Wren. Now I can sleep."

Wren smiled. *I knew she was waiting to hear from me; it's what we do.*

She opened the door. "It's not raining, Rascal. Do you want to go with me to the laundry room to wash dishes?"

Rascal watched while she put the fettucine pot and the rest of the dishes into her dishpan then slipped her hand through the strap on her staff.

"I need two hands to carry the dishpan to the laundry because of the water in the pot; I'll have to take it slow."

When Wren opened the door, Rascal dashed outside while she picked up the dishpan; after she was outside, she leaned against the door with her shoulder and closed it.

That worked.

As she finished rinsing her dishes, a woman came into the laundry. "Is that your dog by the laundry door? He's a sweetheart."

Wren smiled as she nodded. "Rascal likes people."

While the woman tossed her laundry into the washer, she said, "I'll bet he's a good watchdog, too."

"He definitely is."

"I had a golden Labrador Retriever for years; I miss my sweet girl." She smiled. "It must be time to find another companion. Have you been to Jack's Apple Orchard? We heard someone mention them at the gas station and were thinking about going there tomorrow."

"I went there today; you'll love it. They have regular tours that are very popular and a wonderful gift shop; I'm not sure what the hours are."

"I saw the tours on their website; we'll be sure to get there early, thanks."

"Glad I could help." Wren put her dishes in the dishpan, picked it up and balanced it on her hip then headed to the door. When she pushed open the door, Rascal yipped.

On the way back to their camper, Wren said, "After I drop off the dishes, we'll walk around the campground to inspect all the trailers and RVs."

She set the dishpan on the counter. When she joined Rascal outside, he led the way to the far end of their row, then they strolled along each row. When they came to Dana Grace's trailer, Dana Grace was sitting outside with a glass of cider.

"Hey, Wren; if it won't interrupt Rascal's routine, would you care to join me in a glass of cider? The advantage of working at a distillery is that I get to try the latest hard cider flavors. This is Old World Apple Cider."

"That sounds interesting."

Dana Grace put a washcloth over her glass then returned with another glass of cider and a washcloth.

"This is my fancy lid to keep the bugs out." Dana Grace chuckled as she handed the washcloth and glass to Wren. "What's going on with you?"

Wren told her about the podcast in the morning.

"That's exciting; I listen to his podcast; you'll like him."

"I've always written articles for magazines, but I've been working on a novel. I thought I'd read the first part of the novel. Is there something else I should do instead?"

"Your novel's unpublished? The listeners will become your loyal fans because they'll feel like they're part of your 'in' group. What kind of fiction? Do you have a name for it yet?"

"It's a mystery; I've been calling it 'High Falutin' Killers', but I think I may change it to 'High Falutin' Killer' because so far, I have only one killer."

"Either way, love the title; plan on reading at least ten to twelve minutes, so the listeners can get a feel for your style. Do you have a website or a blog?"

Wren sipped her cider. "This is good; it's really smooth, isn't it? I have a brand-new website a friend built for me, and my first blog is there."

"You'll be golden; the last question he always asks every guest is how can our listeners support you and your work? It's a bit of a letdown when people have nothing additional to offer. What's your website?"

"It's called Wrens Twist."

Dana Grace pulled out her phone and tapped. "It popped right up. Your web developer is a marketing guru."

She scrolled through the website. "It's very professional."

Her scrolling slowed. "Your blog is great. How often do you plan to blog?" Dana Grace tapped on her screen. "I'm subscribing to follow your blog."

Wren smiled. "Twice a month. I'm planning to write a flash fiction story for the first of the month and a quick writer's update for the second in the middle of the month."

"You're for sure going to pick up a lot of readers from the podcast."

"How did your day go?" Wren asked as they sipped on their cider.

"Work was busy, but it's Friday; tomorrow will be busier. I'd much rather be busy than sitting around, though. Did you hear about the man from the campground who died?"

"I overheard something in the grocery store, but it sounded a little embellished."

Dana Grace snorted. "I can imagine; Uncle Samuel told me the man was a special agent with the Drug Investigation Division of the Tennessee Bureau of Investigation; my uncle said he had heard there was a sizeable methamphetamine operation in the area."

"I can see how that might be true," Wren said. "It's not like the neighbors across the street can see a lot of strangers pull up in front of a house."

"If there's a task force looking for them, they're on someone's radar," Dana Grace said.

"Which makes them dangerous," Wren added.

"I know; that's what worries me."

Wren sipped her cider to give Dana Grace a chance to explain, but she didn't.

Wren finished her glass of cider. "That was amazing; thank you so much."

"This was one of Uncle Samuel's newest low alcohol content ciders. Some of the rest of them have a real moonshine kick to them." Dana Grace smiled.

"We are in the hills of Tennessee, so while a moonshine kick wouldn't be a shock, this was really pleasant." Wren returned her smile then rose. "I should get back to my camper. I need to go over the questions for tomorrow and stress over what I'm going to say."

"You'll be great, Wren. I listen to the podcast every Saturday. Uncle Samuel assigns someone to cover the cash register for me while I go to the Crafty Artisans room at ten o'clock to turn on the old radio. The room fills with visitors who think they're listening to an old-time radio show."

After Wren and Rascal returned to the camper, she put away the dishes. Wren glared at the pot that went in the outside kitchen cabinet. "There's nowhere to put this except in the microwave, Rascal."

When she stepped outside, she furrowed her brow as she listened to a heated argument between two men in the distance. *Sounds like they're in the direction of the trail but much farther away.*

After she put away the pot, she hurried back inside.

Wren read over the questions before she turned off the lights and opened the blinds next to her bed. After she changed into her pajamas, she lay back and gazed at the bright moon in the clear sky and listened to the barred owl hoot its lonely call.

Chapter Six

At one in the morning, Wren woke to the roar of engines. When she opened her eyes, she was startled by the bright moonlight. *I fell asleep with the blinds open.*

She closed the blinds and sat on the edge of her bed and listened as Rascal whined in his sleep as his feet twitched. *He's chasing something in his dream. Get 'em, boy.*

Wren rose from her bed then padded to the refrigerator and poured herself a small glass of sweet tea. While she sipped her tea, the flashing of her phone screen caught her eye.

She picked it up. *I forgot I'd put it on 'Do Not Disturb.'* She changed the setting. *I missed two texts.*

She opened the texts. *They're from Justin.*

She read the first text that was sent an hour after she dumped her supper into the trash. "I thought you were going to call me back."

She bit her lip as she read the second text that had been sent a half hour ago. "Are you okay? Am I a knucklehead again?"

She smiled as she returned his text. "Yes, and yes. Do we need to talk? Yes."

Her phone immediately rang; she answered, "I love you, so what's your excuse?"

Justin chuckled. "I love you too, honey; I made a huge mistake and listened to bad advice. Your website is fantastic, and I read your blog: it's so you. I could practically hear your voice."

"Remember Gage at the Lonesome Trail Campground?"

"Yes, he and his dad own the campground."

"Right; but before that, he was a big shot corporate marketing director with mad technical and marketing skills; he hated being the boss because he never had the chance to dabble with the technology that he loved. The last question I'm going to be asked tomorrow on the podcast, except now it's today, is how can our listeners support you? The best answer I could come up with was for them to follow my blog on my website."

"Which you did not have." Justin chuckled. "I think I'm catching on now."

"Right; I texted Gage to ask him if he knew anyone who could develop a simple website for me, and he jumped at the chance. He asked me a bunch of questions; we decided I needed a blog, and he had the whole thing set up in an hour, which absolutely blew me away."

"Wow, that's amazing. The website really does fit you; I should have realized only someone that knew you could have designed it."

"He sent me instructions on how to enter my blog; it was a snap. I couldn't have done it on my own, though. Kendra, Gage's mom, is going to be my blog editor; I'm going to blog twice a month."

"This is an excellent foundation for your debut novel," Justin said. "I'm so proud of you."

"So, your turn; why did you go off the deep end over the website?"

"Terry walked into my office just as I opened the link to your website, and she asked me what I was looking at and practically took my phone away from me. She told me it was professionally designed and very expensive and said she was concerned about you being duped out of a huge amount of money. She got me pretty spun up about it, but that's on me; I should have told her to mind her own business. Betsy has been trying to warn me about Terry, but I wasn't listening."

"I went off the deep end when you told me you showed Terry my website, even though I'd never heard her name before. Looking back, it doesn't make any sense, but I thought you and Terry, whoever she was, were buds, and you shared everything about me with her. I was completely offended that she thought she had the right to stick her nose into how I spend my money, and I was really mad at you."

"I finally guessed that part when you hung up on me."

"Maybe you aren't such a knucklehead, after all." Wren giggled.

"Terry doesn't fit in at all in Hidden Gulch, does she?"

"Nope; I think Betsy and a few of her friends are working on that."

"I'll call Betsy in the morning to ask how I can help," Justin said.

"She'll be excited to hear from you and will definitely dream up an assignment for you, but feel free to tell her no because some of her schemes are a little outrageous."

"Are you saying I'll have to remind her I'm the local law when she wants to set Terry's hair on fire?"

Wren giggled. "Exactly, and that might not be very far-fetched; maybe you shouldn't call Betsy after all, so you don't have to arrest her."

"Tell me about your day, honey."

Wren told him about Ruth Whitaker, Dana Grace and Jack's Apple Orchard, the Tennessee Bureau of Investigation agent, the history from the actual owner of the campground, and Ghost warning her away from the old house.

When Wren yawned, Justin said, "Your days make my head spin, but I'm realizing they are just more normal Wren days, aren't they? It's time for you to go to sleep, sweetheart, so you'll be fresh in the morning. Text or call anytime, even if it's just to hang up on me. I can't wait until we're together again; I owe you an I'm sorry kiss for yesterday because I started the whole thing, and I'm so sorry I hurt you."

After they hung up, Wren climbed into bed, closed her eyes, and listened to the comforting sound of roaring engines.

When Wren woke, slivers of light peeked through the trees from the eastern sky. While she started a pot of coffee, Rascal waited for her with his nose against the door. She opened the door;

Rascal dashed out, and Wren shivered then slipped on her flip flops and a sweatshirt.

Rascal cleared the area of any squirrels then grinned as he trotted back to the camper.

After they were inside, Wren poured a cup of coffee and fed Rascal. While she sipped on her coffee, she picked up her phone and shook her head. "I didn't even hear the text that Justin sent after we talked; I must have gone out fast."

She read his text. "Thanks for being the best friend I've ever had. I knew you were mad, but we'd be okay. Love you."

A tear slipped down her cheek. "That's the sweetest thing anyone has ever said to me."

She responded, "You're awesome. Love you so much."

While she sipped on her coffee, she glanced over her questions. "I feel more prepared to answer these questions, at least so far. It will probably help my confidence if I read the first three chapters of my novel aloud. Maybe I should time myself, except I'm not sure if I'll read faster or slower on the podcast."

She exhaled. "I'm glad you'll be with me, Rascal. I'll send the podcast link to Mom because she might like to listen to it if she has the time."

After Wren sent her text, she opened her novel on her laptop. "At least I don't have to look away from my laptop because I won't be reading to an audience that can see me."

She set the timer on her phone and began reading. After she'd finished reading the third page, she stopped the timer.

"I keep stumbling over words. I need to read through this with the idea of reading it aloud first."

While Wren fixed phrasing and word combinations that were difficult to pronounce in the first three chapters, Rascal laid at her feet and closed his eyes.

"I feel better now." She started the timer on her phone and began reading aloud. "'High Falutin' Killer' by Wren Weaver. Chapter One."

After she had read through Chapter One, she glanced at her time. "Have I really been reading for twenty-seven minutes? I guess I got interested in the story, Rascal. Since it's a twenty-minute interview for me on a thirty minute podcast, I should go back and find a good stopping point in the middle of the chapter, except what's a good stopping point? Would it be a cliffhanger or after a certain amount of time? I guess it depends on how slow or fast I read. I'll just ask for a time signal, so I don't have to stress over the time. Thanks for helping me through that, Rascal."

Rascal opened one eye then wagged his tail and went back to sleep.

Wren closed her computer, glanced down, and giggled. *Did I plan to go to the library in my pajamas?*

After she dressed and patted her holster in her waistband, she checked the time. "It's a little after eight, Rascal; I'm going to the registration desk. Want to go with me?"

Wren stuck her phone into her back pocket and picked up her staff. When she opened the door, Rascal stretched then hurried to the door and hopped out as Wren followed him.

When they went inside the registration office, Lorinda smiled. "I'm happy to see you two; how did you sleep, Wren?"

"We slept great; I wanted to tell you how much I enjoyed reading your family history; I think it's too bad Estelle cut out your story about the stock car races, though. Is it okay with you if I include them in my article? People love the idea of staying at a haunted campground, and I can just imagine campground visitors staying outside after dark to listen for the racing cars. Have you thought about building a campground firepit?"

Lorinda chuckled. "Samuel Hudson, who owns Jack's Apple Orchard, and I have been discussing the details of a café for a couple of years that we plan to name Still Secrets Café; we've already met with an architect and a builder, and a lawyer is drawing up a long-term lease. A patio with a firepit would be a perfect addition. I'm sure Sam will love the idea, and our architect and builder will have hissy fits, but they'll get over it and adjust their plans by the end of next week. I've written a brief history of the café that we plan to include on the back of our menu. Would you like to read it?"

"I'd love it; what is your timeline for the café?"

"We have all the permits in place; we'll be ready for our tourist season next spring."

"Would it be okay if I mention the café in my article?"

"You'd do that for us? We'd really appreciate it."

"I did have a couple of questions about the original Whitaker property."

"I'll answer what I can."

"Is anyone staying in the old Whitaker homestead?"

Lorinda frowned. "Estelle and her husband are staying there; I didn't think the house was inhabitable, but she told me they were fixing it up. I haven't seen it yet because she told me she wants to surprise me when it's finished. If I didn't know how well she maintained the campground, I'd be skeptical."

"Is there a driveway to the house? What about the old parking lot for the raceway? How did people get to the raceway, or did they go through the campground?"

"The driveway to the house is just north of here, and it's fairly well maintained, of course, but you'd have to look for it because Estelle's husband took down the mailbox that was alongside the road and opened a post office box in town for their mail. I've never thought about the parking lot for the raceway. It must be on the other side of the campground, but I have the original deed and the hand-drawn map that went with it. I wouldn't mind knowing where that parking lot was myself. Sam, his wife, and I might come up with another joint business venture to pursue."

"I guess I'd better get myself pulled together for the podcast." Wren exhaled.

"You'll be fine; the only people who will hear you are the people who are your friends and the people who want to be your fans. Your enemies will hear only static, thanks to our raceway ghosts."

Wren smiled. "I love the idea; thank you."

As she and Rascal strolled back to the camper, Wren said, "Lorinda said exactly the right thing to cure my case of nerves."

While Wren slid her computer into her backpack, Justin sent a text: "88. That's hugs and kisses in ham radio talk."

Wren smiled and texted her reply. "Love it. 88."

Wren sighed as she picked up her hiking stick. "Let's load up, Rascal."

As they climbed into her pickup, Wren said, "I hope you're ready, Rascal, because I'm not."

As she parked at the library at nine thirty, her eyes widened at the number of cars in the parking lot. "How is this going to work, Rascal? Will I be reading in front of a live audience? What if somebody boos me? Would it be unprofessional if I cry?"

When they went inside the library, Lilibeth, the sheriff, and an elderly man stood near the front desk.

Lilibeth smiled as the sheriff strode to Wren.

"I'm Sheriff Morgan; I received a phone call from Marshal Lewis in Arizona, and after a brief chat, we decided you might need this." The sheriff handed Wren a business card and smiled. "It has my cell number. Call or text me anytime; the marshal said you'd know I can be trusted."

Wren took his card and returned his smile. "He's right."

The sheriff tapped the brim of his ball cap in a salute then left as Wren slipped his card into a pocket on her backpack.

The elderly man extended his hand as Wren continued to Lilibeth's desk. "Wren, it's a pleasure to meet you. I'm Hank, they call me Mr. Radio."

While they shook hands, he continued, "My podcast is called Hankerin' for Radio.'"

Wren smiled. "That's brilliant."

"Welp, you just passed the one and only test for a podcast guest." Hank smiled at Rascal. "This here must be Rascal. He'll be our production assistant today if he'd like to join us. Let me show you where we'll be. Lilibeth has a room that she sets up for anyone that wants to listen. I used to broadcast in front of a live audience, but you wouldn't believe how much coughing, sneezing, loud whispering, and getting up to go to the bathroom goes on until you tell folks they have to be quiet while we're broadcasting."

When they went into the small room, there was a middle-aged, muscular man sitting at a long table near the wall opposite the door. The man wore a headset and was tinkering with the dials on the electronic equipment on the table; the man glanced up then glared at Wren as he removed his headset.

"Wren, this is Philip, my sound engineer; he lives in Chattanooga, but comes here to manage the sound for my podcast; Philip, Wren's my guest today."

"We'll need a sound check," Philip said.

Hank strode to the two square tables with straight back chairs and soft seats that faced each other close to Philip's table then patted the back of a chair. "This is where you'll sit, Wren."

Wren pulled out her laptop and put it on the small table while Hank continued, "Here's your headset; put it on, and we'll talk with our headsets on, so it will feel natural for you."

Hank said, "When we start, I'll ask you the 'tell us about you' question first."

"I jotted down a few notes for all the questions in case my mind goes blank," Wren said.

After Wren had her headset on, Hank said, "Notes are perfect; too many people try to write a script, but that just makes them nervous. This is just you and me chatting. I might interrupt or guide a little to help you out. What do you plan to read?"

"I'd like to read ten minutes from my unpublished novel. I think that will be about half of the first chapter."

"Do you have your stopping point marked?"

"No, because I'm not sure how fast or slow I'll read. Can you give me a wave or something when I'm reaching ten minutes?" Wren asked.

"I need a sound check, Boss," Philip growled.

Hank glared at Philip before he turned to Wren and smiled. "He's right, Wren; that's the best way to do it. Open up the document on your laptop and read your title page to me, so Philip can adjust the sound."

Wren read the title and the first paragraph; Philip continued to frown at the electronic box in front of him, so Hank motioned for her to continue. When she neared the end of the page, Hank held up his hand for her to stop, and she continued reading the paragraph she'd started then stopped.

"I need a hard stop," Philip mumbled.

Hank said, "That was perfect, Wren. You picked a natural point to stop. If I wave my hand in front of my throat, that's a hard stop. Let's practice. Read the next page."

As Wren read, Philip raised his hand; Hank motioned the cut across his neck, and Wren immediately stopped.

Philip nodded.

Hank said, "That was perfect. I think we're ready. We've got about a minute before we start; do you have any questions?"

"How did you get into podcasting?"

Hank laughed. "You know what? Let's end the podcast with that."

Philip stared at the oversized clock that hung over the door then turned a dial on the black box next to him; Wren smiled at the bright fiddle music that was Hank's intro.

Hank waited a few seconds then as the music faded, he said, "Here we are again, folks. You're tuned in to Hankerin' for Radio. Today we have a brilliant journalist with us, Wren Weaver. Wren, tell us how you happened to make your way to Dearheart, Tennessee."

"I love camping, and I'm a journalist on assignment for a travel magazine; so far, I've written two articles about campgrounds: one in Arizona and the other in Texas. Bootleggers Creek Campground is my third campground. My traveling companion is Rascal; he's a black and tan Lab with the curved tail of a Husky."

"Where do you go from here?"

When Wren giggled, Hank grinned as she replied, "I'll find out after I turn in my article for Bootleggers Creek; my publisher likes to surprise me."

"Doesn't that bother you?" Hank asked.

"As long as I'm camping and writing, I can let him have his fun."

Hank chuckled. "You've written only magazine articles that are travel-related, so that's nonfiction. Are you sticking to nonfiction?"

"I'm broadening my writing skills by writing a murder mystery. It isn't quite finished, so it isn't published yet."

"An unpublished mystery? Can you read some of it to us?"

"I'd love to. Ready?"

"Hit it, Wren." Hank grinned.

"'The High Falutin' Killer' by Wren Weaver, Chapter One."

After fifteen minutes, Hank held up his hand, and Wren finished reading the paragraph.

"Wow, Wren. Your story really grabbed me. What are you thinking about for a publishing date? How can our listeners keep up with your progress?"

"I have a website; it's called Wrens Twist. The link is www dot wrens twist dot com."

"Wrens Twist is all one word with no punctuation, is that right?"

"Exactly. I have a blog, and I'll blog twice a month. I'm writing very short stories the first of every month, then in the middle of the month, I'll blog about my writing: what I'm working on and my progress."

"Do you have a name for your blog?"

"Briefly Told."

"I can't wait to follow your blog. Write this down everybody: wrens twist dot com. I don't know about the rest of you, but I can't wait to read 'High Falutin' Killer' by our own Wren Weaver. We've got about a minute left, Wren. Do you have any questions for me?"

"How did you get into podcasting?" Wren asked.

Hank belly laughed. "Now that's an outstanding example of what you can expect from Wrens Twist. Thanks for listening and hug your friends. See you next Saturday, Lord willin' and the creek don't rise."

Hank's theme song played then faded before Philip turned off the electronics.

"That's it," Philip said.

After Hank pulled off his headset, Wren removed hers.

"How are you feeling, Wren?" Hank asked.

"That went fast."

"Think you'd do another podcast?"

"It depends on the host; if I run into someone who is as good as you, I will."

Hank chuckled. "Let's go see what the room of listeners thought, then you may want to head out because they will mob you."

When they walked into the large room with people sitting at tables, a man called out, "That could have been an hour-long special, Hank."

Hank nodded. "I agree. Folks, this is Wren Weaver. Let's give her a big hand."

Everyone applauded, and those who could, rose to their feet. Wren smiled at the sight of the elderly Miss Ruth, who had her hand on her heart while she beamed with pride as she soaked in the sounds of appreciation for Wren's work.

After Lilibeth calmed down the cheers, whistles, and applause, Wren said, "Thank you so much."

"You were awesome, dear; we're all going to sign up for your blog," a woman said.

"We need to let Wren go, so she can stay on schedule with her writing," Hank said.

Wren smiled and waved, then she and Rascal hurried to her pickup.

Trooper Benson was parked next to her pickup. "I caught some of Hank's podcast. Your novel sounded interesting; are you a trained investigator?"

"Not at all; I love to research, and unusual crimes interest me."

Trooper Benson nodded as he strode back to his cruiser. "Thought so."

After Wren and Rascal were in the pickup, she said, "Mr. Hank made it easy, didn't he? He's definitely a master at interviewing; I felt like we were sitting around chatting with our headsets on."

Before she left the parking lot, her phone rang; she quickly parked and answered Justin's call.

"Did you hear the podcast?" she asked.

"Did I ever! I felt like you were in the room right next to me. You were amazing, sweetheart, and you were so smooth when you read your book. I got so caught up in the story, I was shocked that it was time for the podcast to end because I wanted to hear more. You'll have to check your blog when you get back to the camper; I'll bet you already have more than just my comment that you'll want to approve and respond to; that was smart of Gage to set it up like that. Where are you?"

"I'm sitting in the library parking lot; Mr. Hank and the librarian set it up, so that I could scoot out right after I met with the group at the library that listened to the podcast in a large room."

"I want to hear everything about it, but I'll talk to you later; be safe, honey."

Wren smiled as she pulled out of the parking lot and headed toward the campground. "I didn't even think how excited Justin would be to hear my voice; what a wonderful bonus, but I can't tell you how relieved I am that the podcast is over. I might do another podcast but not anytime soon."

When she reached the camper, her stomach growled. "I don't think I ate breakfast. I guess it's close enough to lunchtime that I can have a sandwich while I check my blog."

Before she went inside, a movement near the restrooms startled her; when she turned to look, a man disappeared around the corner to the back of the building.

I'm not used to seeing anyone around during the day. Wren rolled her eyes as she went inside the camper; after she fixed a quick sandwich, Wren sat in front of her computer and read, approved, and replied to comments on her blog.

Her eyes widened as she read a comment that wasn't like any of the others. "Too bad about your podcast being nothing but static, but I guess small town podcasts don't have much of a reach."

Wren raised her eyebrows at the commenter's name: 'TM, Teacher.'

Chapter Seven

Wren sent Betsy a quick text. "Does Terry's last name start with M?"

Betsy responded immediately. "Yes. Did you see my comment on your blog?"

Wren quickly scrolled and found Betsy's comment: "So proud of you."

Wren approved it and responded, "Love your support."

She texted Betsy. "Yes, read it and replied."

Wren spent the rest of the morning replying to texts and approving and responding to comments on her blog.

"It's a big splash, Rascal; I won't see this every time I blog, but it's a fantastic response to get me energized. I'm ready for a break; want to walk to the registration office to talk to Lorinda?"

When Wren and Rascal went into the registration building, Estelle was behind the desk; she glanced up then glared. "Is there a problem?"

"Not at all; we were on a walk and just thought we'd drop by to tell you how beautiful the campground is."

Estelle's face softened. "I work really hard on it; I like for things to look nice. People sure can make a mess, can't they? But I guess if we didn't have any people around, we wouldn't have a campground; at least that's what Mama keeps telling me. I remember you; you're Wren Weaver, and you're related to the Williams on your mama's side. I'm Estelle."

"Hi, Estelle. I thought you had gone to Chattanooga for the weekend. I'm sorry you had to cut your weekend short."

"'Preciate it; I don't get away much, so it was a big disappointment when my husband said I had to come back to make sure the campground was okay. I didn't see what he was so fired up about; it's Mama's campground, not his."

Wren scanned the room. "Where is Miss Lorinda?"

"Since I was back and could fill in, she went to a meeting with my dad's cousin and his wife. Mama's always looking for ways to improve the business at the campground. She's a very smart businesswoman." Estelle beamed.

Wren blinked. *Estelle is being sociable; should I be scared or relieved?*

"She certainly is; I guess we'll continue our walk."

"Stop by anytime," Estelle said. "Oh, wait a minute. I forgot my manners. What's your dog's name?"

"Rascal."

Estelle pulled out a dog treat from a drawer. "Here's a treat for Rascal; he's a handsome dog."

Wren and Rascal headed to the desk, then Wren stopped. "Why don't you give it to him? He'd enjoy that."

"Me? I don't know how."

"Tell him to sit then give it to him. He'll take it very gently from you because he knows you're new at giving treats, and he doesn't want to scare you."

"Okay." Estelle swallowed hard then cleared her throat. "You ready, Rascal?"

Rascal walked close to her; Estelle glanced at Wren who smiled and nodded.

Estelle held out the treat and closed her eyes. "Sit."

She peeked with one eye then slowly gave it to Rascal who just as slowly and gently took it from her.

"Well done," Wren said.

Estelle exhaled. "Thanks."

She smiled at Rascal. "Thanks for the training, Rascal. I don't know why, but I've always been afraid of dogs. Mama wanted one when I was little, but I threw such a fit, she didn't get one. I'll have to tell her I'm sorry. Stop by again. Mama keeps dog treats here, but I never knew why."

As they continued their walk, Wren said, "That was a surprise; she was almost pleasant and quite chatty. I wonder if it's because I'm related to the Williams on Mama's side or because I complimented her work?"

After they'd walked past each trailer and RV on the campground, Wren said, "Let's go back to the camper; I'll write the article for the Bootleggers Creek Campground then send it to Betsy and maybe Kendra for editing, so I can send it to Charlie tomorrow. Wouldn't it be nice if we could leave on Monday?"

While she was typing her article, her phone buzzed a text from her mom. "I'm so proud of you, sweetie. You were awesome on the podcast. Dad and Ellie thought so too."

Wren's eyes widened. "Mom sent the link to Ellie. If I'd known that before the podcast, I would have totally frozen and been completely unable to squeak out one word."

She resumed typing her article; after Wren was finished, she re-read it and made a few changes. "Okay, Rascal. I've done what I can. I'll send this to Betsy and to Kendra for comments. Both of them will be polite and try not to hurt my feelings, but they'll let me know if they find anything."

After she sent the two emails with her article attached, Wren said, "Would you like to go for a walk on the trail then to the raceway? Maybe we can find the parking lot and the driveway from the main road to the parking lot."

Rascal stared at her as she stuck her phone into her back pocket.

Wren slipped on her gaiters that served as snake boots then tightened the leg straps before she headed to the door with her hiking staff. "You don't have to go, but I don't think it would hurt for you to give up part of your afternoon nap for some fresh air."

After they were outside, Rascal dashed ahead. Wren chuckled. *He's pretending it was his idea all along.*

As she headed to the trail, Wren noticed Chester Hudson as he came out of the storage room next to the laundry. He quickly ducked behind the building and disappeared. *I thought Estelle said she returned by herself. I might have misunderstood.*

When she reached the trail, Wren listened to a mockingbird, a cardinal, and brown thrashers sing their songs. *No rain today.*

Rascal and Wren continued on the trail past the point where they'd gone into the woods to the raceway. *I think we're going around the raceway. This is a beautiful walk.*

When the trail stopped, Wren peered through the trees on her right. "Do you see that wooden building, Rascal? Could that be the concession stand?"

Rascal led the way through the trees to the shack with walls of broken, decayed boards with newer planks added across the old boards to shore up the sides and a partially caved-in roof with a tarp over it. Next to the building was a large propane tank with peeling paint.

As Wren stepped carefully through the high grass toward the building, she wrinkled her nose at the overwhelming odor of urine. *There must be a bear or a bobcat in the area. I'll take a quick look then head back.*

She hurried to the side of the building that had a wide opening that faced the raceway; the bottom of the opening was chest high and had an eighteen-inch ledge of splintered wood with the perfectly round holes that were the signature of carpenter bees. She snapped a photo of the front of the concession stand then a side view that didn't include the tarp. *I might blog about this sometime.*

When she stepped to the side of the building where the tarp was over the roof, she stood near the doorway but stayed outside when she saw that the floor was littered with signs of mice and roaches. She snapped four different shots of the interior.

Wren peered at the commercial grade gas stove with a huge, rusted pot that spanned across two burners; next to it was a stained and chipped porcelain farmhouse style sink. On top of the counter that was beside the sink were assorted sizes of glass containers and canning jars with a variety of powder, liquid, or solid contents, a large funnel, rubber tubing, a rusted metal strainer, and empty soft drink bottles. The doors were missing from the cupboards underneath the counter. Wren squinted at the containers on the shelves. *I can't really read the labels from here, but I recognize the rusted cans of camp fuel. I'll bet the rest are cooking oil or cleansers.*

One door on the overhead cupboards was missing, but the other four were intact. The cupboard door pulls were decorative cars from the 1920s. *Those are beautiful.* Wren zoomed in and snapped photos of the upper cabinet cars and the one open cupboard with its contents then snapped photos of the lower cabinets to see if the labels would be clear enough to read.

A dented and rusted-out six-foot long chest-type cooler with a missing lid was against the far wall; two buckets and an abandoned nest of paper and insulation was on the floor in the corner near the cooler. Wren peered at the door next to the cooler. *That must be a storage closet.*

A wide pendant light shade with a frayed cord hung from the ceiling over a worktable in the middle of the room that was in relatively good condition compared to the rest of the fixtures. *The worktable looks like it's a later addition. Running water and electricity. This would have been fancy back in the day.*

Wren examined the high weeds and brush around the track. "I think there may be remnants of bleachers around the raceway track, Rascal. Wouldn't you expect the entrance to be near the concession stand, so the customers could buy a beer or a jar of moonshine before the race? Let's see if we can find a walkway or a ticket booth."

Rascal disappeared into the brush behind the concession stand; Wren returned to the trail then trudged into the brush where it had stopped. She intently watched where she placed her feet and examined the surrounding carpet of tangle weeds for snakes as she pushed through the heavy brush; when she reached a section of blackberry bushes with wicked thorns, she stopped. *I'm wearing myself out. I'll go back to see if Rascal has found anything.*

Wren turned around then stared at the thicket in front of her. *Is that the right way? I was too busy watching for snakes; I don't know which way to go.*

She whistled for Rascal then listened for him to bark in return. *I'm too far away from him; he can't hear me.* She pulled out her phone and stared at it. *Great, no bars, and I don't know who I'd call, anyway.*

She whistled again; a mockingbird whistled his tunes in response.

"What are you standing out there in the woods whistling for, doll?" Ghost asked.

Wren peered in the direction of his voice but didn't see him.

"Where are you?" she asked.

"In the parking lot; same as your dog."

"Am I close to the parking lot?"

Ghost chuckled. "Not hardly; you been walking in circles. Me and your dog will come getcha."

Wren sighed and squinted at her phone. *Still no bars.*

She gazed at the treetops and the sky as clouds gathered and exhaled in disgust. *The birds quit singing, and I left my rain gear in my truck.*

Ghost said, "Okay, dog; go get her."

Wren smiled at the thrashing sounds in the brush that became louder until Rascal broke through a thicket and grinned. She knelt as she rubbed Rascal's face with both hands then hugged him and cooed, "Good boy."

Wren rose to her feet. "Thank you, Ghost."

"Doll, you gotta quit getting yourself in trouble; you're wearing out me and your dog." Ghost chuckled.

After Rascal led Wren back to the trail, and they were on their way back to the campground, Ghost's voice sounded like a light whisper in the breeze. "Stay off the road at night, doll."

Wren frowned. "I don't have any plans to go anywhere after dark."

She held her breath in the long, unsettling silence as she waited for Ghost to say more. *Why does Ghost think I'll be out at night?*

She exhaled and shuddered as a swarm of cicadas buzzed, then another nearby set picked up the chorus and buzzed even louder.

"It's definitely going to rain later tonight, Rascal, but I need something for supper and forgot to get anything when we were in town. I'd planned to have last night's leftovers; I definitely wasn't thinking straight when I dumped my food into the trash last night." Wren examined the sky. "We have enough time to go to the grocery store and return long before dark."

On the way to town, her phone buzzed its notification of a text. Before she reached the grocery parking lot, it buzzed a second, then a third time.

Wren grumbled, "I need to either set my phone to do not disturb or take it out of my back pocket when I'm driving."

She peered at her phone. "I have two texts from the same number, and the third one is a different number, but I don't recognize either of them."

She furrowed her brow as she read the first text. "It's D.G. Got your number from your invoice. Call me ASAP."

She read the second text. "This is Lorinda. Dangerous storm headed this way. Shelter at the high school."

The third text was from Dana Grace. "Call ASAP."

Wren called Dana Grace.

Dana Grace answered on the first ring. "Where are you?"

"Grocery store parking lot."

"I'm at the campground; come back, so you can follow me to Uncle Samuel's house. We're going to get slammed by a severe storm in about an hour. It was supposed to be a normal, heavy rainstorm, but it's blown up."

"On my way."

Wren turned toward the road. "It's daylight, so Ghost won't be mad at me, and the road's straight; hang on, Rascal, we have to go back to the campground." Wren sped as fast as she could on her way back to the campground.

When she arrived, Dana Grace was waiting in her truck next to Wren's camper.

"Grab what you can, then let's go," Dana Grace said as Wren pulled up.

Wren jumped out of her truck, ran inside, and tossed her two drawers of clothes and the contents of her laundry basket into an oversized tote bag before she picked up her computer bag. On her way out the door, she snatched up Rascal's bag of dog food.

Dana Grace said, "Let's go; they live on this side of the orchard, so we're not that far away. Stick close."

The sky in the west was dark, and streaks of lightning jumped from cloud to cloud followed by low rumbles less than a minute later. Wren stayed as close to Dana Grace's bumper as she dared. When Dana Grace signaled a turn, Wren slowed then followed her up a driveway to a house on a hill.

After they parked, Wren opened the door for Rascal. While Wren pulled out her backpack and computer bag, Dana Grace opened the passenger's side back door and removed Rascal's dog food and the tote full of Wren's clothes.

As they walked toward the house, Dana Grace said, "Bootleggers Creek is expected to flood if that storm hits us straight on, which is what the forecasters are saying. The sheriff's deputy arrived in a van at the campground when I did; he's taking campers to the high school. You'll be more comfortable here, and so will Rascal. Uncle Samuel and Aunt Virginia have a storm cellar, but so far, there have been no reports of strong winds or radar indications of a tornado with the storm. I was listening on the radio, and the storm has slowed, which makes it even more likely that the creek will flood."

"I need to let Lorinda know I'm here; she sent me a text to go to the high school." Wren sent the text before they went inside.

A middle-aged woman with streaks of gray in her dark-brown hair smiled as they entered. "Wren, I'm so glad to meet you, even if it's not under the best of conditions; I'm Virginia. Dana Grace, show Wren where to put her things." Virginia took the dog food from Dana Grace. "I'll put Rascal's food in the utility room."

As Dana Grace led Wren to her bedroom, she said, "Our bedrooms have a jack and jill bathroom between them. The house was a bed and breakfast when Uncle Samuel and Aunt Virginia bought it, but Aunt Virginia said after she looked into all the regulations, she decided she'd just host family."

"I'll need to call Justin to let him know what's going on."

"Oh, of course; I'll get the lowdown on Justin later, right?" Dana Grace smiled.

"Just like I'm going to get the lowdown on the elusive husband." Wren's eyes twinkled as she smiled.

Dana Grace closed the door to the bathroom then closed the bedroom door as she left. Wren sat on the Queen Anne chair in the corner and called Justin.

"Good timing, Wren. My last meeting of the day ended, and I'm catching up on paperwork. How are you doing?"

"I'm at the house that belongs to the owners of the apple orchard. Their niece was staying at the campground and told me we have a storm coming that is expected to flood the creek and the campground, so Rascal and I came here."

Justin exhaled. "I'm glad you told me, but I'm really sorry you had to evacuate the campground. Did you have time to grab your laptop?"

Wren smiled. *He's so practical.* "Yes, and I dumped all my clothes into a tote bag and grabbed Rascal's food on the way out. I just realized I didn't get his treats, my hairbrush, or my toothbrush. I put the box with all of Miss Miranda's stories on the back floorboard of my truck earlier because I kept tripping over them in the camper."

"Maybe the campground won't flood, but I know you'd have hated to lose Miss Miranda's stories."

"I can't believe you had Saturday meetings; what's that all about?"

"Two old friends of mine from the academy stopped by; they're in the Arizona Department of Safety Criminal Investigation Division. We went to lunch and got to talking; one thing led to another, and the whole day was gone."

"That's the State Police, right? Are you thinking about becoming a crime investigator?"

"Just kind of kicking it around; what do you think about it?" Justin asked.

Wren frowned as she listened to the torrential rainfall as it pounded against the windows and the roof. *I'm really glad I'm here and not in the camper or a shelter. What if the shelter didn't allow dogs? Rascal and I would have stayed in the truck or tried to get to the Copper Kettle Diner.*

"I think it sounds like something you'd want to do."

"I kind of wondered ..."

Dana Grace lightly tapped at the door.

Wren interrupted him. "Just a second."

Dana Grace opened the door and peeked in. "Sorry to disturb you, Wren, but the food is on the table. No rush; Aunt Virginia just wanted you to know."

"Thanks," Wren said.

After Dana Grace quietly closed the door, Wren said, "I'm sorry, but they're holding supper for me. I'll try to keep you updated on the storm. Love you."

She hung up then hurried to the kitchen. When she entered the kitchen, she inhaled the tantalizing aroma of chicken and spices.

"I made chicken and dumplings," Virginia said. "It's my version of comfort food during storms; the rain is deafening, isn't it?"

While they ate, Dana Grace asked, "Did you bring your phone charger, Wren? It's a good idea to fully charge your phone in case we lose our electricity."

"I didn't think of it, but I'm fairly certain I have a spare in my computer bag. I should charge my laptop too."

"You girls can plug in all your electronics after we eat, then we'll have apple cobbler with a scoop of ice cream and a smidgeon of apple brandy sauce," Virginia said.

After they finished eating, Wren said, "Thank you so much, Mrs. Hudson. I've been eating prepackaged meals for almost a week; the chicken and dumplings were wonderful."

"Glad you enjoyed it, but if you can't call me Virginia, Wren, then call me Aunt Virginia. When you say Mrs. Hudson, it reminds me of the doctor's office."

Wren smiled. "Okay, Aunt Virginia."

Samuel stood near the back door. "Ready for an after dinner dash, Rascal? Let's go outside for a breather before it gets any worse."

After Samuel and Rascal disappeared in the deluge, Wren and Dana Grace hurried to their rooms to charge their phones.

When she reached her new bedroom, Wren pulled out her chargers and her laptop from the computer bag then plugged in her phone and her laptop.

Dana Grace came into Wren's room from the bathroom. "Aunt Virginia keeps the bathrooms stocked for company, so if you forgot your toothbrush, shampoo, or any other toiletries, help yourself. There's a small closet in the bathroom with a wide selection. Just take what you need, and Aunt Virginia will be thrilled."

When they went into the kitchen, Rascal was stretched out near the stove.

Samuel said, "We have no TV and no internet, but the local radio is already talking about flooding and advising people to leave the low-lying areas if they can do so safely."

"They won't be able to leave at all in half an hour; they need to get out now," Virginia grumbled.

"Some people don't want to evacuate because they think the forecast is an exaggeration, or they can protect their homes if they stay." Samuel shook his head. "I'm really glad you and Wren are here, Dana Grace."

Rascal nudged Samuel's hand; Samuel chuckled. "And Rascal."

"I haven't fed him," Wren said. "Where is his food?"

"He might not be very hungry because he was my taster for the chicken." Virginia's eyes twinkled. "His food is in the pantry." She pointed to a door.

"He might have considered that his appetizer." Wren smiled as she found his food. "I didn't pick up his food or water bowls; do you have something we can use?"

"I already set down water for him." Virginia pulled out a plastic bowl from a cabinet below the countertop. "Will this one work?"

Wren's eyes widened. *That's a dog bowl.* "That's great."

After Wren fed Rascal, she furrowed her brow. "I can't imagine being on the road in this."

Samuel stood at the window near the back door. "It would be impossible to see. The smartest thing to do would be to find a place to stop where no one would hit you. There are a few roadside parks along the roads, but you'd have to know where they were because no one could see them in this rain."

Lightning flashed and was immediately followed by a crash and rumble of thunder that was drowned out by the boom of an explosion; the lights went out.

"From the sound of it, I think we lost a nearby transformer." Samuel turned on a flashlight; Virginia set a kerosene lantern on the table then lit the wick.

"I'd like to write; is it okay if I bring my laptop in here?" Wren asked.

"Of course, it is." Virginia opened a drawer then handed Wren a small flashlight. "Here you go."

Wren hurried to her bedroom then returned with her computer. While she sat at the table and wrote, Virginia dished up four servings of apple cobbler and ice cream then drizzled applejack brandy syrup over the ice cream.

Samuel and Rascal came inside from the back door; Samuel removed his shoes, rain slicker, and hat, but before Rascal could shake water all over the kitchen, Samuel grabbed a towel.

While Samuel rubbed down Rascal to dry him, he said, "It's rough out there; the rain is still heavy, and now the wind's picking up. We moved your car to the shed, Virginia."

He flipped the light switch next to the back door, and the kitchen lights came on. "I got the generator going, so we can have lights and water from the well before bed. I'll turn it off before I hit the sack."

"Thanks, honey; I enjoy parking near the trees for the shade; I didn't think about moving it when we heard about the storm." Virginia put the ice cream in the freezer then extinguished the kerosene lantern. "Dessert's on the counter; serve yourself."

When Samuel peered at the four servings, Virginia pointed to the one with the most cobbler. "That one's yours, honey."

While they ate their dessert, Virginia asked, "Is your article about the Bootleggers Creek Campground finished, Wren?"

"It's being reviewed by my editor and a beta reader, then I'll send it to the publisher."

"I've got a family story for you," Samuel said. "It's not anything you could use in your article, though, but if you ever need it in one of your novels, go ahead."

Wren smiled. "I'm not touching the article except for making the editing changes from my reviewers, so I can certainly promise you that I won't add it to the Bootleggers Creek article."

Samuel returned her smile. "You may have already heard some of this. Every family has skeletons, and the Hudsons are no exception. Clarence Whitaker and Norman Hudson were rivals when they were in high school; when Clarence Whitaker married Norman Hudson's longtime high school sweetheart, the rivalry turned to bitterness. Except for A.J., Norman's sons amplified their dad's rancor and passed it on to their sons, who didn't know why they had a grudge against the Whitakers, but they hated them. Andrew Jackson Hudson was more like his mama's side of the family who were farmers in Alabama. Those Alabama farmers didn't have any use for feuding with neighbors. You either got along, or your farm would fail and your family starve without the neighbors that stepped in if you needed help."

"Of course, A.J.'s brothers thought he was a traitor," Virginia added.

"When World War II broke out, all of Norman's and Clarence's sons were drafted. In a strange twist of fate, Norman's sons returned, but all of Clarence's sons were killed in combat, leaving him with three grandsons."

"The youngest grandson was George Whitaker, but they called him Ghost because he drove his car so fast and with such skill that he couldn't be caught," Virginia said. "Anyone care for coffee, hot tea, or hot cider?"

"Coffee for me," Samuel said.

"I'd like hot cider," Dana Grace said.

"I would too," Wren said.

"You already know A.J. bought the apple orchard when he returned from the war; his two brothers went into competition with their dad's old rival, Clarence Whitaker. The Hudsons, I'm embarrassed to say, cut corners in the quality of their moonshine to the point of poisoning people with bad batches of 'shine that should never have been sold," Samuel said.

"Sheriff Cooper would have been glad to have busted their still," Virginia said.

Samuel chuckled. "We have to be careful what we say around you-know-who because she's got sheriff's blood running through her cynical veins."

Virginia snickered as she swatted his arm. "And don't you forget it, fella."

Samuel continued, "The two Hudson brothers spied on Clarence Whitaker, so they could predict when he was going to have a big batch for Ghost to run to Nashville for Clarence's best and most feared customer. They knew which way Ghost would go to Nashville because Ghost shied away from any major roads. One brother waited for him near one of the worst hairpin turns on his route then rammed Ghost from behind."

"They knew Ghost could control his car and even outrun him, so they had a follow up to their plan," Virginia said.

Samuel nodded. "The other brother waited at the hairpin curve and stepped out into the road in front of Ghost's car."

"Wasn't he taking a terrible chance of being run over?" Wren asked.

"They knew Ghost would take his car over the drop off before he'd harm someone."

"Wow; they were counting on his skill as a driver and his kind heart."

Samuel nodded. "The two brothers bragged about sending Ghost into the ravine. They told old Clarence Whitaker they'd taken care of Ghost, and they'd take care of the rest of his family if he didn't quit bootlegging. Clarence believed them; he visited A.J. late that night, and the two of them dismantled Clarence's still and moved it to one of A.J.'s storage sheds."

"Two nights later, the brothers went to Clarence's still to take it and were incensed that it was gone. They murdered Clarence, tossed his body into a ravine, and bragged about it."

"With Clarence and Ghost gone, they expected to pick up Clarence's customers, but their reputation for tainted product was too well established. They turned to manufacturing drugs, but their business was cut short after they were drafted; both of them died in the early days of the Vietnam War."

"Wow, what a story. How much of it do you think is true?" Wren asked.

Samuel shrugged. "It's hard to say because that side of the Hudson family likes to revel in the reputation of being the 'bad boys' that hoodwinked the law; don't ask me why."

Virginia smiled. "It's probably about ten percent true, but it's a great story to be told during a storm while we're safe and dry. More coffee, Samuel? Girls, more hot cider?"

"I wouldn't mind another cup, honey."

Wren shook her head, and Dana Grace said, "We're fine."

After Virginia refilled Samuel's coffee cup, the two of them went into the family room.

"I have a book to read," Dana Grace said, "if you'd like to have some time to write, but first, tell me about Justin. You were on the phone quite a while."

"He's the town marshal in Hidden Gulch, Arizona."

"Friends or more?" Dana Grace asked.

"More than friends," Wren said.

"Arizona? Did you meet him when you wrote your first article, or did you already know him?"

Wren smiled. "Your turn to tell me about the elusive husband."

Dana Grace smiled. "I'll give you the official version because you'll read between the lines and understand; just like I understand about Justin. His name is Max, and he's a long-distance trucker. We haven't been married all that long, so the family here hasn't met him."

Wren nodded. "He's like Justin."

Dana Grace raised her eyebrows. "You're quick; you're going back to Arizona after you complete your next assignment, aren't you?"

"That's my plan," Wren said.

"Thanks for understanding, Wren; I'll get my book."

While Dana Grace read, and Wren wrote, Wren received a text from Kendra. "Loved the article. Check your email for a couple of minor changes."

Wren rose from her seat and stretched. "My editor said she's sent me a couple of minor changes. I may be able to send my article to the publisher when the electricity and the internet service are restored."

"Good news, except I hate to see you go, Wren," Dana Grace said. "I don't really have any friends here, so it's been nice to have someone to talk to without creating suspicion because I dodged a bunch of questions."

"I can't tell you how much I appreciate that you thought of Rascal and me when you heard about the storm."

Later, Virginia came into the kitchen. "I'm setting up the coffee for the morning. Any breakfast requests?"

"Biscuits and gravy," Dana Grace said.

Virginia chuckled. "I don't know why I bothered to ask. You are certainly your dad's daughter, Dana Grace. He always asks me to make biscuits and gravy."

Wren yawned, then Dana Grace yawned.

"You're too old for me to tell you to go to bed because you're tired, but I can mention that it's my bedtime." Virginia smiled as Samuel came into the kitchen.

"Rascal and I will go outside for a quick break," Samuel said. "Honey, we have to get a dog because Wren will probably insist on taking Rascal with her when she leaves."

Samuel and Rascal went outside into the pouring rain.

"Our sweet old dog, Lady, died three months ago, and neither one of us has mentioned getting another dog," Virginia said. "Lady and Samuel were really close."

That's why they had the dog bowls and why Rascal is sticking close to Samuel.

After Samuel came inside, he dried Rascal with the fresh towel that Virginia gave him. "I'll go back out in a few minutes to turn off the generator, but I'll give everyone time to get ready for bed first."

When Wren and Rascal went to her bedroom, Wren said, "I'll leave the door open a crack, so you can leave if Samuel gets up before we do."

Dana Grace opened the bathroom door. "You can have the bathroom first, Wren. I'm going to wait until morning to shower because we might have electricity by then."

Wren pulled out her pajamas and took them into the bathroom. After she found a drawer with new toothbrushes sealed individually and toothpaste, she selected a toothbrush with a red handle and brushed her teeth. She opened the linen closet and smiled at the four styles of new hairbrushes; she picked one and opened the packaging then brushed her hair. After she washed her face and put on her pajamas, she cracked open the bathroom door to Dana Grace's room. "Your turn; goodnight."

"Goodnight, Wren; hopefully we'll have electricity tomorrow."

Wren hurried into her bedroom and closed the bathroom door behind her. She turned off her light and climbed into bed with her phone and called Justin.

"I'm really glad you called, sweetheart; I was getting worried."

"I've never seen rain this heavy before; we lost electricity, but Mr. Hudson has a generator, so we've had lights. I charged my phone and computer."

"It's still raining?"

"Yes; we're under a flood warning, except the Hudsons' house is on a hill. I'm certain the campground will flood, but I can't guess how much. How's your day been?"

"Oh, you know, I'm living the carefree bachelor life."

Wren smiled. *I'll bet this is good.* "Really? Another beer bust with adoring models fighting for your attention as they hang onto your every word?"

"Very close to that; I did the laundry, including folding and putting it away, went grocery shopping, and mopped the kitchen floor."

Wren giggled. "You're so funny."

"I'm really glad you're in a safe, comfortable place. How's Rascal doing?"

"He's living the life. Mr. Hudson takes him outside then rubs him dry with a fresh towel when they come back inside; Mrs. Hudson told me that Rascal was her taster, so he enjoyed bites of chicken before supper. The Hudsons' old dog passed away a few months ago; Mrs. Hudson said Rascal is helping her husband to recover from his loss."

"They sound like wonderful people."

"They really are. I heard from Kendra. She said she had a few editing changes for my Bootleggers Creek article, but since we don't have internet, I can't download what she sent me. We're hoping for electricity and internet tomorrow."

"Kendra is Gage's mother, right? After you put in her changes, will you send it to your editor?"

"You're right, she is. I forget sometimes that you only know people in Texas because I've told you about them. I don't know whether I've heard from Betsy yet; she has a particularly keen eye for words and phrases that might not work for readers."

"Did you think about what we talked about earlier?"

What did we talk about earlier?

"You mean the Arizona State Police?"

"What do you think?"

"I think it's a good fit for you; you're too talented to be spending your time in meetings and paperwork."

"But what about you?"

"I'm too impatient to be in meetings."

Justin exhaled. "We have a major disconnect here. I won't be in Hidden Gulch."

"Of course, you won't." Wren frowned. "The flood warning might have stressed me more than I'd like to admit, but I feel you're saying something that I'm not hearing."

"I'm so sorry; I didn't even think of that. The thing is that I've seen how much you enjoy traveling to new places and meeting new people, but then I worry you wouldn't want to leave Hidden Gulch because you have friends here, so maybe you really wouldn't want to go somewhere else."

"What? I got lost. Why wouldn't I..."

Justin interrupted. "We can still be good friends and text and talk on the phone like we do now, can't we? I don't want you to feel like I'm trying to pressure you or anything. Maybe this whole thing about criminal investigation is a bad idea. I don't have to leave Hidden Gulch, you know; maybe I'll just stay here after all."

Wren rolled her eyes. "What if I absolutely insisted on going with you? Would that be okay, or would you need time to think it over?"

"What? You'd want to go?"

"I'm in Tennessee, and I was in Texas last week; in case you haven't noticed, I'm pretty mobile. When did you put in your application for the state police?"

"Quite a while ago; how did you know?"

"Nobody would ever just stop by Hidden Gulch. Was it an interview?"

"More of a pre-orientation."

"When did they let you know you were accepted?"

"When they called to say they'd like to stop by. I've been worried about what you would want to do since you left for Texas."

"That's terrible; why didn't you say anything?"

"I was afraid you might say you'd always be my friend."

"That's crazy talk because I will always be your friend; why would that hold you back? I'm excited for you. When are you giving notice to Hidden Gulch?"

"Oh, okay; friends travel together all the time, don't they? I had to talk to you first, so I'm glad we could finally talk. I have to give notice on Monday, so I can be in the next orientation class. They're held only twice a year, which is why the guys wanted to talk to me."

"We'll figure it out."

"Right, but for now, you need to concentrate on what you'll be doing the next few days. Let me know."

"I will."

As they hung up, Samuel headed down the hall toward the kitchen. "Lights out, literally."

The distant hums from the kitchen appliances were silenced, the glow of the computer charger darkened, but the rain raged on.

Wren pulled up the covers and fluffed the pillow until it was the way she liked it. She sighed as she relaxed in the comfort of being safe from the storm and closed her eyes.

I wonder why Justin really applied for the job with the state police. I'll focus on him, not the storm, the next time we talk.

Chapter Eight

Wren woke enveloped in silence and a suffocating blackness. She reached for her phone, but all she felt was her bed that had mysteriously and ominously become wider and more yielding overnight. The soft surface that wasn't her bed terrified her as she realized she had slowly sunk into its deceptive trap. She threw off the covers in a panic to escape from the terrifying dark then exhaled with relief. *I'm at the Hudsons'.*

She moved to the edge of the bed then felt around the small table until she found her phone. When she picked it up, the bright screen lit her corner of the room. *Five o'clock isn't too early to get up; I can write until everyone else wakes.*

She quickly dressed, including slipping her pistol inside its holster then opened her bathroom door. *Dana Grace's door is still closed.* She grabbed her hairbrush and brushed her hair then used her phone light as she opened her bedroom door.

She inhaled the aroma of coffee and smiled at the glow of the kerosene lantern coming from the kitchen at the end of the hallway.

When Wren tiptoed down the hall and into the kitchen, Rascal greeted her with a grin when he saw her and trotted to her; she set her laptop on the table then hugged him.

"You're up early," Virginia smiled. "Thank goodness for a gas stove and an old percolating coffee pot from our camping days. Ready for a cup, or do you want to wait a bit?"

"Now, please."

"No limp this morning, I see. Are you giving up your hiking stick?"

"I think if I don't stress my ankle and reinjure it, I'll be fine."

Virginia poured a cup for Wren and refilled her own then joined Wren at the table.

While Wren waited for her coffee to cool, Virginia said, "I listened to the radio earlier. The system finally moved on, and the rain stopped not long ago. At least from the early reports, we have more areas underwater than the forecasters expected."

"Not just flooded, but underwater?" Wren furrowed her brow.

"That's what they're saying, but we won't really know until daylight."

Samuel came into the kitchen. "I didn't expect anyone to be up so early. Any of that coffee left?"

"About a cup and a half." Virginia poured a cup for Samuel while he put on his jacket.

Samuel drained his cup. "Rascal and I will do a quick check around the house then start the generator."

Virginia poured the rest of the coffee into Wren's cup. "The noise of the rain got me up at four; it finally stopped about half an hour ago. What woke you so early?"

"I'm not sure, but I was really disoriented by the dark because I thought I was in the camper."

While Virginia set up the coffee maker for the next pot, the clocks on the coffee maker, the stove, and the microwave remained dark. When the clocks flashed and the dishwasher and stove beeped, Virginia chuckled. "It's official: our kitchen appliances are pleased to announce that the generator is on."

The coffee maker gurgled as it heated the water to brew its first morning pot.

When Samuel and Rascal came inside, Samuel scraped his feet on the mat while Virginia refilled Samuel's cup with the freshly made coffee.

Samuel dished up food for Rascal. "We have some trees down, and our yard's a mess, but we don't have any damage to the house; one tree took out part of our fence behind the house, and another one hit the old shed, but none of them are blocking the driveway. All in all, we're in pretty good shape."

While Samuel fed Rascal, he asked, "When's breakfast? What's the latest news?"

"Early reports are a little sketchy; a reporter talked about areas being underwater. If you'll get some bacon going, I'll mix up a batch of biscuits."

Samuel chuckled. "Biscuits and gravy, of course; Dana Grace is here; I'll turn on the radio first, though."

Samuel went into the family room where they had been listening to the radio the night before and brought it into the kitchen. "I've switched it off battery power." He set it on the counter then plugged it in.

While the radio announcers discussed the rain and speculated about damage, Samuel pulled out the bacon from the refrigerator while Virginia set a frying pan on the stove then began gathering the ingredients for biscuits.

Dana Grace was barefooted as she wandered into the kitchen; she was still in her pajamas and hadn't brushed her hair. She squinted at the brightness in the kitchen. "What got you all up so early?"

"Biscuits and gravy," Samuel said.

Dana Grace whirled around. "I'll be right back."

Virginia chuckled. "You certainly have a way with words, honey."

After they ate breakfast, Wren opened her laptop and squinted at her screen. "I think the internet service is back."

Dana Grace peered over Wren's shoulder. "Sure is; the password is apple flowers with no space between the two words."

Samuel said, "If the internet's up, I'll bet the electricity is too. I'll turn off the generator, and we'll see when I switch the electricity back to the power company."

Samuel and Rascal went out the back door. After the lights went out, the electronic clocks on all the appliances went dark too.

A few seconds later, the lights came back on, and the time on all the appliance clocks began flashing.

"We have electricity," Virginia said. "I wish the coffee maker had a battery or something to hold the time like alarm clocks do. It's a pain to reset." She reset the time on all the clocks.

Samuel and Rascal came back inside. "It's getting close to sunrise; I'm going to the orchard after I do a few things here."

"I'd like to go with you, but I want to rinse the pinto beans I soaked overnight and pop them into a slow cooker first," Virginia said.

"I'm smart enough to never argue when food is involved," Samuel said. "Is it okay with you if Rascal rides along, Wren?"

"His choice." She smiled; Rascal grinned.

"We'd like to check the campground sometime today too," Dana Grace said.

Samuel nodded. "That makes sense; if you'll wait until after we get back from the orchard, we can go in my truck. It's heavy duty and has four-wheel drive. I don't drive through water, but we won't get stuck in the mud."

Wren had emails from Kendra, Betsy, and Charlie. She rolled her eyes and read Charlie's brief email first.

Wren giggled as she read Charlie's email. "The RV CEO said he appreciates our help with his designs. Please take a picture of your camper at the campground and send it to me. He'd like to have it for a marketing campaign."

"Shall I scramble a mess of eggs?" Samuel asked.

"Be my guest," Virginia said.

"What's funny, Wren?" Dana Grace looked up from her book.

"My publisher has such remarkable timing. He wants a photo of my camper at the campground, so the manufacturer can use it in an ad."

Dana Grace laughed. "There are so many hilarious ways to respond to that email."

"I know, right?"

"You girls are terrible." Virginia chuckled as she stirred the gravy.

Dana Grace's eyes twinkled. "We know."

Wren opened the email from Kendra. Her eyes glistened as she read the kind note from Kendra. "You and Justin will always have a place to stay in Dry Creek. Love from your Texas relatives."

She opened her article then the attachment from Kendra and quickly made the four corrections as Samuel and Rascal came into the house.

Virginia set the biscuits in the middle of the table along with a big bowl of gravy. Samuel set the platter of bacon and the bowl of scrambled eggs next to the bacon.

After coffee refills, everyone dug in.

Wren ladled gravy over her biscuits and eggs. "This is a gourmet breakfast; thank you so much."

"My favorite," Dana Grace added.

Samuel nodded.

After everyone ate, Wren and Dana Grace took over the kitchen cleanup duties.

"Ready to go, honey?" Samuel asked.

"One second; I need to change into my boots and grab a jacket."

After Virginia returned to the kitchen, she left with Samuel and Rascal.

Wren opened Betsy's email then grumbled after she read it. "Marshal Lewis downplayed a few key details."

"What were they?" Dana Grace.

Wren jerked her head up to peer at Dana Grace who had set down her book and was staring at Wren.

"What was what?" Wren asked.

"The few details that were downplayed by Marshal Lewis. Is that Justin? Are we mad at him?"

"I didn't realize I said that out loud; I think we might be. It's too early to call him to yell at him, but I'll read you what Betsy said in her email."

"Betsy's the manager of the campground in Arizona, isn't she?" Dana Grace asked.

Wren nodded then read a section of Betsy's letter to Dana Grace. "Justin's buddies showed up to nag him about the State Police. They visit at least twice every year and try to talk him into joining them. The three of them went through rookie training or whatever it's called either before or after Justin's wife died; I'm not sure of the timing, but when our previous Hidden Gulch marshal needed to retire, Justin came here on a temporary basis until they could find someone else willing to take over. I'm probably telling you something you already know, but he was surprised that he liked it here. Butch heard Justin's two buddies talking at the gas station before they left town. Butch said one man said he was certain they had finally convinced Justin to join them at the state police, but the other man laughed and said he was wrong because they'd been trying to convince him for years, so there had to be a woman behind Justin's abrupt change of mind."

"I'm completely lost," Dana Grace said. "Does that mean you changed his mind?"

"That's what it sounds like, doesn't it?"

"I thought you were looking forward to going to Hidden Gulch; so, have you changed your mind?"

"No, I'd tell you the entire story, but it's even more unclear and convoluted than this is."

"Sounds like Justin is exactly like my husband: a kind-hearted, talented, protective man with a strange, irritating flaw when it comes to understanding his nearest and dearest."

"Does your husband have an oddly insecure side that tries to second guess what you want because I'm thinking this is what Justin is doing."

"Don't get me started."

"I'm going to call him."

"Call him from your room; if you need backup, just throw open your door, and I'll channel my inner Aunt Virginia; she'll set him straight."

Wren giggled. "That's the best plan I've ever heard."

When Wren went into her room, she made her bed then gathered her dirty clothes, folded them, and stacked them on the dresser in her room. She considered taking a shower then snorted. *Excellent procrastination session; make the call.* Justin answered on the second ring.

He sounds exhausted.

"You sound as tired as I feel; did you get any sleep last night?" she asked.

"A little," he said. "More accurately, a little to none. What about you?"

"We stayed up until Dana Grace and I were on the verge of collapse; I woke at five this morning, but we didn't have any electricity; I was really disoriented for a minute or two. Virginia said it quit raining about a half hour before I woke."

"Is there any flooding?"

"Probably. Mr. and Mrs. Hudson went to their orchard to check it, then Mr. Hudson will take Dana Grace and me to the campground after they get back."

"I need to talk to you about the State Police."

"That's good; I'm not half out of my mind from being worried about the storm now. I'm really sorry about last night; the noise impacted me more than I realized."

"I know; I'm really sorry about that. The only excuse I have is I wasn't thinking straight, either."

"We were a mess." Wren giggled.

Justin cleared his throat. "It's not anything I've ever told anyone before..."

"You don't have to now, if you don't want to, Justin."

"I have to tell you. I applied for the position with the state police before Ashley died. She wasn't happy about it because she didn't want to leave Phoenix. After I finished the last two classes, she told me she wasn't leaving Phoenix, so I asked the county marshal to rehire me." Justin's chuckle had a hollow sound. "He promoted me."

"Ashley and I had an argument the night she died. She packed a bag and told me she was going to her sister's. The next time I saw her, she was dead in my arms in the middle of the highway. We had good days and bad days, but mostly bad days, and I always blamed myself."

"Can you tell me what you want to do?"

"It doesn't sound very exciting, but I love my job at Hidden Gulch. I enjoy the administrative and the management sides because there is so much variety; I have new challenges to tackle every day. Pat is a great right-hand man, I have two experienced deputies, and our newest deputy is green, but he's willing to learn; I couldn't ask for a better team. The technical work gets boring really quickly, at least for me; it's much more mundane than people realize. I'd love to travel for vacations, but I'm not interested in working in a city. Your turn; I'd like to hear what you want to do."

"I love to travel and meet new people, but I'm not looking to travel all the time. I'm used to having roots where I know people and have friends."

Justin chuckled. "That's obvious: look at the friends you've made in Texas and now Tennessee."

Wren smiled. "Kendra sent me her editing comments for the Tennessee article and in her email she said that you and I will always have a place to stay in Dry Creek, Texas, and signed it love from your Texas relatives."

"She included me? I'd like to visit Dry Creek," Justin said. "So, where does that leave you and me?"

"As far as I'm concerned, nothing's changed except I love you even more. I'm going to my next assignment, then Rascal and I are headed straight for Hidden Gulch."

"Good; that means I can relax and not stress over selling my house."

"If you want to leave, you can leave, but I'm living in your house, so it won't be lonely."

"That's an excellent idea."

"You're going to leave?"

"No, you're going to live in my house, so it won't be lonely. What about your camper? Have you heard anything about whether the campground flooded?"

"We haven't heard anything, so maybe everything is fine; that's why we want to check it for ourselves. Dana Grace has her in-laws' trailer there."

"What about your Bootleggers Creek article? I'm trying to catch up on everything; can you tell?"

Wren giggled. "See, that's why I don't understand when you try to hint stuff because you usually just flat out tell me. I have Betsy's comments to look over, then I can send the article to Charlie."

"Then the fireworks begin." Justin chuckled.

Wren snickered. "You don't know how true that is. Charlie sent me an email yesterday sometime, and I read it this morning after the internet came back online. He wanted me to send him a picture of the camper at the campground, so the manufacturer would have a photo for an ad."

Justin laughed. "You're going to do it, aren't you?"

"Absolutely, if we can get to the campground. Mr. Hudson said he doesn't drive through water at all, and he has a large truck with four-wheel drive."

"He's smart; we always have several drownings when there's a flash flood in the mountains, and the water rushes down the arroyo. People just don't understand the force that water has."

"What's an arroyo?"

"It's like a ditch; it's dry most of the time, but it's caused by the water from a heavy, upstream rainfall. I'll show you."

Wren sighed. "I'm so glad we talked."

"When are you going to send your article in?"

"It probably won't take me more than a few minutes to take care of Betsy's corrections, but I want to see the campground and the surrounding roads before I send the article to Charlie. If the campground is fine, I could leave as early as tomorrow, but I'd tell him Tuesday, so I don't have to rush."

"I know his email didn't give you any sign of where your next campground is, or you'd have already told me."

"You're right; what are your plans today?"

"Sheridan invited me to help him work on his latest project at the campground, and Socorro enticed me with tamales, so that's probably what I'm doing."

Wren exhaled. "There aren't any tamales around here."

"That's too bad; you'll have to come here for tamales."

Wren smirked. "It's a pretty good reason for me to return to Arizona."

"Among others."

Wren smiled. "I love you, Justin; I need hugs and kisses for putting up with you."

Justin laughed. "Touché, honey. Love you so much."

After they hung up, Wren sighed. *How am I getting to the next campground with Rascal if my camper is ruined?*

When she strolled into the kitchen, Dana Grace looked up from her book. "I don't mean to be nosy, but you aren't crying or throwing things, so tell, boss lady."

"Justin didn't want to leave Hidden Gulch; he thought I might miss traveling and would feel stuck in there, but he never asked me straight out. We had an excellent discussion with no crying; I didn't think about throwing anything; it's not a bad idea in case of emergencies."

"My favorite misunderstandings are the ones that are solved after a good night's sleep," Dana Grace said.

"You really nailed it; last night, both of us were exhausted and not thinking straight. Have you heard anything about the orchard?"

"The driveway to the orchard, the parking lot, and the store are fine, so I'll be able to open on time tomorrow. There was a little water on the road between here and there, but not much. Uncle Samuel is doing a quick drive in his utility vehicle around the orchard to see how many trees he lost; Aunt Virginia said it wasn't as many as he feared, at least from what they could see from the driveway."

"Good." Wren opened her laptop. "I'll get Betsy's comments in, then the article will be ready to go, but I'm not sending it until we know the condition of our trailers."

Dana Grace exhaled as she rubbed her forehead with her fingertips. "I'm really worried about the in-laws' trailer; I'm sure they have insurance, but I feel responsible."

"Could you have hooked it up in the three minutes you gave me to pack my things?"

"I'm certain you took at least four; however, point taken." Dana Grace smiled.

After Wren finished her article, Dana Grace asked, "What happens after you send in your article?"

"In theory, the publisher gives it to an editor who makes any adjustments needed for the space available in the magazine by working with the formatter; after the layout for the entire magazine is completed, it is published online and sent to a printer according to the schedule. We'll see how things go this round."

"That's in theory; so, how has it gone for the past two articles?"

"Stop me anytime because it's a sad, dull story. The editor is a frustrated, no-talent writer and has no interest in editing. He completely rewrote my first article because he didn't like the main character that was the same as the local legend, so I asked the editor to pull my article and take my name off the article the editor wrote, or I'd quit. It was practically the same story with the second article. I expect the same this time too. That's why I have my own editor and beta reader because I can't allow it to be published without being edited."

"I don't understand your publisher. How can he allow an incompetent editor to stand in the way of publishing delightful articles that are being enjoyed by more and more people?"

"The publisher is the editor's uncle; I suspect the editor has worn out his welcome in the publishing world, and his uncle may be under pressure from the rest of his family."

"What a mess." Dana Grace shook her head. "I'm glad you're going to blog, though. What are your plans?"

"After my fourth article, I'm resigning from the magazine and won't be writing any more articles for them. I agreed to the four-part series, so I'm going to see them through."

"Unless you quit." Dana Grace's eyes crinkled as she smiled.

"Of course. What about you? What are your plans?"

Chapter Nine

"Max has mentioned shifting his career to something that isn't so behind the scenes after his current project is finished, but he's so good at what he does, I think he wouldn't be happy," Dana Grace said. "Things have worked out fine for us because I can work at the orchard, and we had our time together at the campground. We'll have to see what we can work out."

"I think Uncle Samuel and Aunt Virginia would never mention to anyone that they had an additional guest at the house," Wren said.

Dana Grace furrowed her brow. "No one in the family around here knows we're married or even that he exists."

"Uncle Samuel is the grandson of Andrew Jackson Hudson, who was trusted by one of the most talented bootleggers of all time, and Aunt Virginia is the granddaughter of a respected sheriff. You and Max will be safe."

"You have such a different way of seeing things; I like it. I'll run it past Max and have an off-the-record conversation with Aunt Virginia and Uncle Samuel."

"A possibility is that we talk to Virginia and Samuel together; maybe I'm the one with an undercover person named Justin. It would be a way to feel them out."

"We could do that. I'll check with Max; he'll be apoplectic, but he'll get over it." Dana Grace grinned.

"Best case is that the campground didn't flood, and we just had an interesting hypothetical discussion," Wren said as Samuel opened the door, and Virginia and Rascal came inside.

Rascal hurried to his water bowl and took a long drink.

"Rascal insisted on going with me and ran the entire way. I couldn't coax him into the utility vehicle to ride," Samuel said.

"He's always been like that; maybe it's his Husky side that runs with the sled."

"I didn't think about that; I was worried about making an old dog run, but he was loving it."

Wren giggled. "Old? He's only four."

Samuel shrugged. "Maybe I'm the old dog that couldn't have run it, so I worried about him. Are we ready to go?"

"I'm staying," Virginia said. "I have a lot to catch up on, including baking."

"Ready, girls? Are you going, Rascal?"

Rascal trotted to the back door.

"I'll ride in the back with Rascal." Wren opened the door for Rascal then climbed in next to him.

On the way to the campground, Wren gazed at the flooding along the swollen creeks and the litter of toppled trees caused by the saturated ground that could no longer support their roots against their heavy, rain-soaked leaves.

She stared at a wooden bridge over a creek at the bottom of a hill that had been partially washed out by the now-ebbing flood.

Wren said, "Dana Grace, do you see the baby goats splashing in the puddles next to the small house at the top of the hill?"

They'll rebuild their bridge and be okay.

Dana Grace peered out her window. "Baby goats have the right idea, don't they?"

After they crested a hill, the severity of the flooding of the campground came into view. The ditches along both sides of their elevated road left debris of leaves and sticks on the road as signs of the extent of their overnight overflow that was slowly receding.

As they neared the campground, only the top half of the campground sign was visible, but the sign had wet leaves and mud caked on it above the waterline, which left evidence of how high the flood reached during the night. Samuel crept past the driveway that was barely recognizable under several inches of murky water.

"Would it be safe to stop for a second, so I can take a quick picture?" Wren asked.

"As long as you don't get out of the truck." Samuel stopped the truck in the middle of the road.

Wren quickly lowered her window then snapped a photo of the sign and a second one of the driveway.

"Thanks." Wren raised her window.

"The campground is going to be a mess," Dana Grace whispered.

"I don't see any reason to go into town this early." Samuel turned around in the middle of the road and headed back to his house.

"Now what, Wren?" Dana Grace asked.

"I'll send my article and the picture of the campground sign to my editor. I don't think I'll be going anywhere tomorrow."

"Wren, you're welcome to stay with us as long as you like," Samuel said.

"Thank you; if my editor doesn't come up with anything reasonable, Rascal and I will head toward Arizona on Wednesday."

"How are you going to do that without a trailer?"

"I'll get a tent and a sleeping bag; I can plan a two-day stop in Dry Creek, Texas, and spend a night or two with Kendra while I do laundry and sleep in a bed before I go on."

When they returned to the house, Virginia asked, "How was the campground?"

"Underwater," Samuel said. "The campers won't be salvageable at all."

"You two are welcome to stay here as long as you like," Virginia said, "but I'm sure Samuel already told you that. What will your plans be, Wren?"

"Don't mean to interrupt, but do we have any cookies, Virginia?" Samuel asked. "We need to celebrate the fact that we're okay and dry."

"Good idea; it won't take me long to mix up a fresh batch."

"I'll start another pot of coffee." Dana Grace rinsed the coffeepot. "Wren, send your email to your publisher then we'll catch up Aunt Virginia on all our tentative plans."

Wren nodded as she opened her laptop. After she sent the document and the picture of the campground sign to Charlie along with an explanation, she sent the campground sign photo along with a text to Justin: "I'll let you know what Charlie says." She sent a second text with the submerged driveway.

While Dana Grace poured coffee, Wren showed Virginia the two pictures she'd taken.

"I don't see how either of their campers would be salvageable," Samuel said. "The electronics would be fried, and the floors and walls would have to be ripped out and replaced. All that would be left would be their tires and the metal frame."

"Good grief; it's almost unbelievable, isn't it? That would be very drafty, and not very comfortable for sleeping." Virginia put the first batch of cookies into the oven.

Dana Grace smiled as she glanced at Wren. "Sleeping under the stars, literally."

Wren giggled. "A camper's dream."

Wren sipped her coffee. "We'll see whether Charlie comes up with a way for me to complete my final assignment. If he ignores the flood and the fact that the camper is gone, I'll quit and return to Arizona."

"How long would that take you? I've heard there are hotels that accept dogs, but it seems to me they have a weight limit that an old cat would exceed," Virginia said.

Samuel chuckled. "Rascal's a smart guy, but I'm not sure he could fake the twenty-pound or whatever it is weight limit."

"Before Mom and Dad got a trailer, we camped in a tent with our sleeping bags, so that would be fine for Rascal and me. We'd stop in Dry Creek, Texas, at least for an overnight or two. Rascal and I could be in Hidden Gulch in four or five days, depending on how long we stay in Dry Creek."

"That's not a bad plan." Virginia pulled out the first batch of cookies from the oven and put them on a plate before she slid the next batch in to bake. "So, we wait, right?"

Wren's phone buzzed a text from Justin. "Unbelievable. Call when you have time."

Wren said, "Justin wants me to call him when I have time."

"Since we're not planning to go bail out our trailers yet, you probably have a little time, don't you?" Dana Grace smiled.

As Wren rose to go to her room, Virginia pointed at the plate of cookies in the middle of the table. "Take one for the road."

After Wren grabbed a cookie and munched on it as she headed to her bedroom, Rascal trotted along behind her.

She kicked off her boots and fluffed her pillows then climbed onto her bed. Wren leaned back against her pillows and called Justin.

He answered immediately. "Those were unbelievable photos. Were you able to check your camper?"

"No, we might go back later. I see why Samuel said he didn't drive through water; its depth is very deceptive. I sent my final article and those same pictures to Charlie. We'll see what he has to say."

"So, how are you going to get to your next assignment if you can't take your camper?"

"That's Charlie's problem. I think I might be ready to leave here by Wednesday. I don't know how to explain it, but I feel like there's unfinished business here for me to take care of before I leave."

"Related to Ghost?" Justin asked.

"I don't know; maybe."

"I went by to check on Thomas earlier; he wanted to know when the annoying bird girl would be back."

Wren snorted. "He knows my name; he's just being his usual irritating self."

"Which is why he asked me to tell you what he said." Justin chuckled. "What kind of camper do you think the RV manufacturer will have for you to evaluate next?"

Wren smiled. *He's more relaxed.* "So far, the campers have been for a solo traveler with barely enough room for a four-legged companion. I'd like to try out something big enough for a couple or at least a higher end trailer for a solo traveler."

"Do you think the CEO has a price ceiling in mind?"

"Maybe, but none of the trailers I've had would be comfortable enough for a cross-country trip or even an extended vacation at the beach or the mountains; they're only acceptable for weekend camping."

"I was kind of poking around looking at fifth wheels; I'll send you a video of one I found online."

"Are we shopping for a camper?" Wren giggled.

"Somebody has to; your RV CEO's heart is probably in the right place, but he doesn't seem to have much imagination, does he?"

"You're going to be our camping expert before long."

"There's an RV show in Tucson next week; Sheridan and I will probably go."

"Those are so much fun," Wren said. "Mom, Dad, and I used to go to RV shows when I was little. I came home with large bags of what Mom said I called nifty items."

"Nifty items?" Justin laughed.

Wren giggled. "Mom said one of the sales guys told me he had a nifty item for me, and I must have either loved whatever it was or the words."

"I'll pick up some nifty items for you at the show."

"That would be awesome."

Wren paused when she heard Dana Grace speaking in the kitchen. "I'll go along, Uncle Samuel, and check with Wren."

"I think Dana Grace has something to tell me. Is it okay if we talk more later?"

"Sounds good to me."

Wren hurried toward the kitchen; Dana Grace met her in the hallway.

"Uncle Samuel has to go to the orchard to do a few things before we open tomorrow. I'm going; would you like to go too?"

"I'd love it."

"Do you have any work gloves? We'll probably be dragging limbs to clear the trail for the tour bus," Dana Grace said.

"I do in my truck; I'll grab them when we leave."

"Should Wren and I take my truck or hers, Uncle Samuel?" Dana Grace asked when they went into the kitchen.

"Wren's truck might be best. Yours has a bigger engine, Dana Grace, but her tires would have better traction in mud."

"Are you staying with me, Rascal?" Virginia asked.

Rascal cocked his head at Samuel.

"What do you think, Wren?" Samuel asked.

Wren rolled her eyes. *Samuel doesn't want to be the bad guy.*

"How wet is the ground at the orchard?"

"It's still like here, not too swampy," Samuel said.

"It's your choice, Rascal," Wren said.

Rascal trotted to the back door.

"I'll make a big pot of chili while y'all are gone and a special treat for Rascal," she said. "Take some water with you; you'll need it, and so will Rascal."

Dana Grace stuck three bottles of water into her backpack before they left.

On the way to the orchard, Wren gazed at the fallen water level in the ditches alongside the road. "The flood water's gone down a lot."

"It usually does; the water flows downhill but soaks into the ground along the way, so the valleys won't flood any worse than they already have."

When they joined Samuel on the gift shop porch, he said, "John Andrew is out there working, but he could use some help. Do you think you two could take one of the four-wheel drive utility vehicles and use straps to drag the branches off the trail? John Andrew could use our large tractor with the grapple to haul the branches to our burn pile to dry out. Right now, he's doing both."

"We could do that," Dana Grace said.

While they checked the straps in the back of the utility vehicle, Wren asked, "Who's John Andrew?"

"He's the son of one of Aunt Virginia's close friends or cousins; I don't really know him or his family. I think Aunt Virginia and his mother have been good friends since they were teens. He just graduated from high school and has been working in the orchard; I think he's going into the military next month. Uncle Samuel likes him a lot because he's such a hard worker, gets along with everyone, and is a natural-born mechanic; according to Uncle Samuel, there isn't a piece of equipment that John Andrew can't fix."

"Who's driving? You or me?" Wren asked.

"You drove here, so I guess it's my turn to drive."

Rascal ran down the trail in front of them then stopped at the first set of branches across the road.

Dana Grace wrapped one end of the strap around a large branch while Wren connected the other end to the hook on the back of the UTV. After Wren checked the strap around the branch to be sure it was tight, Dana Grace jumped into the driver's seat while Wren and Rascal stepped far enough away to avoid being hit by the strap if it snapped.

Dana Grace dragged the large branch away from the road then backed enough to loosen the strap. "That's one." Dana Grace grinned.

After they moved the other two branches, they headed for the next obstruction on the trail with Rascal in the lead.

They moved at a steady pace and cleared the trail in less than two hours.

After they returned the UTV to the equipment shed, Wren pulled out Rascal's collapsible water bowl, and Dana Grace gave Wren two bottles of water. Wren poured one bottle into Rascal's bowl; Rascal quickly drained his bowl while Wren and Dana Grace sat on the gift shop porch and sipped their water.

When Samuel joined them, he said, "I appreciate your help; John Andrew would have been here half the night making sure the trail was cleared for the tour bus."

After he left, Wren asked, "Are you ready to go back?"

"I have a few things to do in the gift shop; you don't have to hang around, though."

"I'd like to drive by the campground to see if it's still underwater," Wren said.

"I'd love to go too, but if I left, Uncle Samuel might mess up the gift shop in the spirit of trying to help." Dana Grace chuckled.

"I'll see you back at the house; let me know if you want me to come get you."

When Wren reached the campground, the driveway was dry, and even the ditches on the sides of the driveway had very little water in them.

As she approached the registration office, she narrowed her eyes at the large puddles around the building. After she made the turn toward the campsites, she sighed and called Justin.

"Are you okay, Wren?"

"I'm fine. Rascal and I are at the campground registration office. I can't go any closer to the campsites because the roads are too muddy, and I'm afraid I'll get stuck. From the amount of mud and debris on the sides of the campers and RVs, I'm guessing the floodwater reached three feet."

"They'll all be declared total losses because their floors would have been underwater. Is there anything in the camper you'd like to salvage when you can get to it?"

"The air fryer, my coffee maker, and favorite pan aren't close to the floor; I wouldn't mind having them."

"You might want to call the Waco RV dealership, so they can get an insurance adjuster there; you don't have to wait for the insurance adjuster to take any of your personal items, though."

"Dana Grace and I can come back later this afternoon to see what we want to remove from our campers. I'll call her now; I'll talk to you later."

Wren called Dana Grace and told her about the campground and the level of water. She added, "We can come back later this afternoon to salvage what we can."

"Uncle Samuel might want to come with us; I'll let him know what you found."

After Wren called the Waco RV dealership where she had picked up the camper, she and Rascal climbed out of the truck to see if they could walk to the camper.

As they walked toward the camper, Wren said, "Let's walk to the row behind our site; it looks a little higher and drier."

When they reached the camper, Wren said, "Rascal, stay here; there's no reason for both of us to have muddy feet."

Wren slowly stepped through the mud. "Don't fall; don't fall," she muttered. She unlocked the camper and shook her head. "There's still water on the floor."

She went inside and pulled out her air fryer from the cabinet and picked up her pillow. She dropped her hairbrush, shampoo, scrubbie, and shower soap into the pillowcase. Wren sighed. "This is all I can carry at once; I'll make a second trip for my kitchen items."

After she emptied her pillowcase onto the front seat and set the air fryer on the floor, she returned to the camper with the pillowcase. She filled it with the kitchen utensils, her favorite pan, and two pots that she loved then closed the camper door and locked it. She set her pillowcase on top of the air fryer.

"Want to look around a bit, Rascal? I'd like to take a peek at the restrooms."

After she unlocked the door to the ladies' restroom, she peeked inside. "Water intrusion here, Rascal; I'll bet the septic has been flooded, so it won't be just a matter of cleaning the restrooms."

She closed the door. "Want to see how far we can go on the trail?" She smiled. "Can you tell I've felt kind of stuck inside?"

When they reached the trail, it was underwater. "The creek is still flooded."

Wren peered at an unusual object that was partially submerged about ten feet from where she stood. "Can you tell what that is, Rascal? It's large, but it doesn't look like a tree. Maybe an appliance?"

Rascal growled then barked. Ghost stood next to Wren. "Yer dog's right; it's a dead man, doll."

"Wow, did he drown?"

"You might call it that, but he got himself a little case of lead poisoning first."

"He was shot? Who was he?"

"No kin of mine." Ghost disappeared.

"My backpack is in the truck, Rascal. Let's call the sheriff."

"Good choice." Ghost's voice floated from the treetops.

Wren and Rascal climbed into the truck, and she locked the doors as she called Sheriff Morgan.

"You need help, Wren?" the sheriff asked when he answered.

"Rascal and I came to the campground, and we found a man facedown in a pool of water."

"Be right there; are you safe?"

"We're in my pickup, and I locked the doors."

"Don't leave your truck."

Chapter Ten

"I couldn't tell who he was, Rascal, could you?"

Rascal whined.

"I guess I could call Justin while we wait for the sheriff."

Justin answered immediately. "I know something's wrong; are you safe?"

"Yes, Rascal and I are in my pickup with the doors locked. We're at the campground and found a dead man facedown in the creek overflow; I called the sheriff, and he's on the way here."

"That's good; he gave you our code words, didn't he?"

"Yes, he said call or text him anytime, but I don't understand why I was supposed to call him, not nine-one-one."

"Precautionary; there's an ongoing investigation there that has nothing to do with you, but you're there, so you have everyone nervous."

"I don't understand," Wren said.

"You have a way of drawing out rats from hiding."

"You're trying to tell me something without saying too much, but I'm not getting it at all; does this have anything to do with Terry?"

"That I can answer. No, this has nothing to do with Terry."

"Am I safe at the Hudsons'?"

"Yes, you can trust the Hudsons and Sheriff Morgan."

"But no one else, except Ghost."

"For now, that's correct, but it's all precautionary."

"I just realized how you knew something was wrong; it was because Thomas told you, wasn't it?"

"Yes, and did you notice we're having a strange conversation?" Justin chuckled.

"No, I didn't; we seem to have conversations along this line regularly." Wren giggled.

At the sound of a car engine, Wren glanced at the driveway. The sheriff sped down the driveway then slid to a stop next to Wren's pickup.

"The sheriff's here. Love you," she said.

"T or c anytime. I love you, honey."

After they hung up, Wren and Rascal climbed out of the pickup.

"Can you show me where the body is, Wren?"

Rascal led the way to the trail. After they reached the trail, Wren held her breath. *The body better not be gone.*

When they reached the edge of the overflow, the sheriff narrowed his eyes as he examined the body. "Drowned?" he asked.

"You may find he's been shot."

When the sheriff stared at her, Wren added, "I have a feeling."

"Wren, I have to ask you not to tell anyone about this. As far as anyone's concerned, I came to the campground to check it out and found the body. Got it?"

"Dana Grace and the Hudsons already know I was coming here."

"Fine; you came here, checked your camper, and left. I came here to check the campground and found the deceased. You know nothing about a dead man at the campground; got it?"

"Got it."

Sheriff gazed at Wren with concern on his face. "Are you sure? It's critical that you understand."

Wren met his gaze. "I don't understand, but I can do it."

Sheriff nodded. "You don't know how much I appreciate that you called me. Where are you going from here?"

"Rascal and I are going to the Hudsons' house."

On the way, Wren said, "I think Justin goes obscure when he drops into lawman mode."

Wren rounded a sharp, blind curve a little faster than usual on her way to the Hudsons' house. An old-fashioned Cadillac was parked hazardously on the shoulder at the curve with its fins encroaching on the roadway. An older woman in the travel lane struggled to loosen the lug nuts on a rear flat tire. The sunlight caught her silver hair and gave her a delicate aura that made her predicament even more heartrending.

Wren pulled onto the shoulder. "Stay in the truck, Rascal; you'll be safe here."

When Wren approached the woman, she asked, "Could you use some help?"

The old woman wore a long-sleeved shirt and worn leather gloves. Sweat trickled from her hairline and into the lines of worry and age etched on her face. Her breathing was labored as she looked up at Wren. "I haven't done this in a very long time."

"Let me see what I can do; before I loosen these lug nuts, can I see your jack?"

The woman frowned. "That should be in the trunk; I've been so afraid someone would come around the curve and hit me that I haven't been thinking ahead."

Wren tried to open the trunk. "I think it's locked; do you have the key?"

The woman frowned. "I just had it."

Wren glanced toward the driver's seat. "Could your key be in the ignition?"

"I'm not thinking straight at all; after I pulled out the tools from the trunk, I closed it and dropped my keys on my seat."

After Wren opened the trunk, her eyes widened. *This trunk is filled with boxes.*

The old woman said, "I think I know exactly where it is."

She pulled out a box and handed it to Wren. "Hold this a minute."

"I expected the box to be heavier," Wren said.

"I couldn't manage them if they were too heavy, could I?" The old woman pulled out a second box. "This isn't going to work at all, is it? Put these two boxes on the backseat; I'm certain the jack must be in this back corner."

"I'm Wren; are you traveling alone?" Wren put the second box on the backseat.

"You can call me Greta; I like to travel alone. Here's another box for the backseat."

After Wren had put the fourth box on the backseat, she joined Greta at the trunk. "Sometimes they put the jack under the mat. Should we lift the corner to see what we can see?"

"No, nothing's there." While Greta moved more boxes around, she dropped a purple velvet pouch with gold trim onto the pavement. Wren leaned over to pick it up, but Greta snatched it up.

Wren's eyes widened at the woman's quick reflexes. Greta's smile didn't reach her eyes. "Just some old jewelry with sentimental value."

"I can call for some help," Wren said.

"No, I'm rested now. If you'll put the boxes back into the trunk for me, I can take it from here."

Wren bit her lip as she put the boxes back into the trunk, and Greta slammed the trunk closed then locked it. *It doesn't feel right to leave her here alone.*

Wren exhaled in relief when a cruiser with its emergency lights flashing pulled in behind Greta's car.

"Lord, no; not him," Greta muttered.

"Do you live nearby, Wren?" she asked.

"I'm staying with friends, just up the road."

Greta nodded. "The Hudsons' are good people. Take this." She turned her back to the state trooper's cruiser and dropped her car keys into the velvet pouch then pulled the gold cords tight to close it before she shoved the velvet pouch into Wren's hand.

"Don't let him see you have it; give it to Sheriff Morgan. If you tell him I gave it to you, he'll know what to do," she hissed.

Wren dropped it into her backpack as Trooper Benson strode to them. "Hi, Wren. You're everywhere, aren't you?"

Trooper Benson stepped to the side of Greta's car and examined her flat tire. "Got yourself in a fix, didn't you, Greta?"

Greta held her hand low and out of Trooper Benson's sight then motioned for Wren to leave.

Trooper Benson narrowed his eyes. "I'll call for a tow and give you a ride into town, Greta."

Wren started moving toward her truck.

Trooper Benson narrowed his eyes. "Thanks for your help, Wren."

Wren smiled. "You're welcome."

When Wren joined Rascal in the truck, she said, "That was bizarre, Rascal. I went from a possible petty thief to a best friend the second Trooper Benson showed up."

After she parked, Wren called the sheriff.

When he answered, she asked, "Do you know Greta? She had a flat tire and gave me a purple velvet pouch to give to you."

"Who knows about it?" Sheriff asked. "Where are you?"

"I'm at the Hudsons'. Trooper Benson called for a tow truck and was going to give her a ride."

"Thanks for the call. Don't tell anyone about the pouch."

He hung up; Wren pulled out her pillowcase with all its kitchen items and her pillow.

Virginia met her and Rascal at the back door. "Dana Grace called me; I called her mother about the trailer, and she'll contact the owners. I have water for hot tea and sweet tea in the refrigerator. Who do you need to notify about your trailer?"

"I called Justin and the Waco dealership. I need to call my publisher."

"You need fortification: hot tea or sweet tea with your cookies?"

"Hot tea after I put some of these things away." Wren raised her pillowcase.

"I have a cardboard box you can use." Virginia put it on the table for Wren.

"I'll take all my things to my room then pack there." Wren picked up the box and took everything to her room.

Virginia called out, "Let me know if you need another box."

"So far, I'm doing fine."

When Wren came into the kitchen, Virginia said, "Back to your hot tea: with or without applejack?"

Wren laughed. "Without for now; maybe with this evening."

After Virginia set the mug of hot tea on the table, she asked, "Do you need to talk in private?"

"No, I might need to vent after I get off the phone."

Virginia put a plate of chocolate chip and pecan cookies on the table then took one for herself.

Wren called Charlie and narrowed her eyes as she waited for him to answer. *He better not let it roll over to voicemail.*

"Hello, Wren. I'm glad you called; I was just about to call you."

Sure you were. "Good timing, then; what were you calling about?"

"I got your email with your article about the Bootleggers Creek Campground. You are definitely the right journalist for these articles. It took me back to when I was a kid, and my dad took me to the stock car races. I can still hear the roar and smell the hotdogs and popcorn from the concession stand. We've got one detail to iron out, but it's minor."

"Minor detail." Wren narrowed her eyes and tapped her thumb on the table.

Charlie cleared his throat. "The editor hasn't reviewed it yet."

"How does that affect me?"

"Well, he's on vacation..."

Wren interrupted. "The article has already been edited by a professional editor and approved by a beta reader, so how does your nephew's vacation impact my article?"

"Oh, so you know it's Blake." Charlie sighed. "I suppose I could just tell the family..."

"Whatever you like, so where do I go for my assignment?"

"We need another week..."

"I only need two minutes to sign my resignation and send it to you."

"You'd quit over a slight delay?"

In a heartbeat. Wren took a bite of cookie. *Time to stop arguing.*

"I could throw in a bonus," Charlie said.

"You probably should throw in a bonus."

"So, we agree: one additional week."

"You'll have my resignation in less than five minutes. I've enjoyed the assignments."

"Wait, wait," Charlie said. "Can I think about this overnight?"

"No. How long did it take you to read the article? Don't you know a competent editor who could read the article and give you a thumbs up or a thumbs down? Get back to me by five o'clock your time; I'll hold my resignation until five oh one."

Charlie exhaled. "There's no other way to do this, is there?"

"No, sir, there isn't: five o'clock."

"I think I can do it." Charlie hung up.

"That was a tense conversation," Virginia said.

"It's a repeat of two others; I've gotten better at cutting out a lot of nonsense."

Virginia smiled. "My favorite quotes are 'You probably should throw in a bonus' and 'I'll hold my resignation until five oh one.' I notice you didn't mention the camper; how was it?"

"I sent him a photo. He said he read my email; he didn't, or he would have asked me about the camper. The campground had about three feet of flood water, according to the watermarks on the trailers and RVs."

"Wow, that means all of them would have had their floors underwater, which would have completely ruined the floors, walls, cabinets, furniture, and probably the electrical," Virginia said.

"I talked to Dana Grace; we might go back later this afternoon when it's a little drier to see what we can salvage. I called the RV dealership in Waco where I picked up the camper, so they could contact their insurance company and get an adjuster here to assess the damage."

"What a mess; you're certainly welcome to stay here as long as you like."

"Thank you. Rascal and I will probably leave Tuesday; it's all up to Charlie whether we head west or east. Meanwhile, I'll write more chapters of 'High Falutin' Killer'. According to my outline, I'm about three-quarters of the way through."

"West is back to Arizona and Justin; east is to your next assignment. I think your readers will be disappointed if the magazine doesn't publish the fourth article."

"I want to do the fourth article, but I don't even know where it is. We'll just have to wait to see what Charlie decides; I've gone through this with Charlie after every article."

"I have a logistics question. How are you and Rascal going to get back to Arizona with no camper?"

"We'll get a tent."

"I may have one in storage that we haven't touched in ages. We can at least check it out before you buy one. After you and I put it up, we might decide to take it to the dump and get you a new one. I think the new ones are a lot lighter than the old ones."

"You're probably right, but the older ones are sturdier; it's a tradeoff, isn't it?" Wren said. "Another option is that Justin might come here."

"He's always welcome too; there's no waiting period for a marriage license in Tennessee."

"We're not quite there yet," Wren said.

"In that case, he's definitely welcome, so we can work on the rest of it."

"He's a lawman, so he wouldn't want anyone to know he was here."

"We don't have any close neighbors, so he could relax and be incognito."

Samuel and Dana Grace came inside.

"We're good to go tomorrow; thanks for the help, Wren," Samuel said.

"I'll have lunch ready in two shakes," Virginia said.

While they were eating, Virginia asked, "You took longer coming back than I expected, Wren. Was everything okay?"

"I came across a woman on a curve with a flat tire. I tried to help her, but I couldn't loosen the lug nuts, and we couldn't find her jack. Her name was Greta; do you know her?"

Samuel and Virginia gave each other The Look.

Wren furrowed her brow. *What did I miss?*

"Tell her," Dana Grace said.

Virginia nodded. "Greta has been the biggest drug dealer in the county for years. I've always thought she either knows where all the skeletons are or has the entire county on her payroll."

"She has been a devoted supporter of our kids' baseball team, which makes her a hero," Samuel said. "She's an interesting person because she doesn't allow any dealers to sell to the kids in our county."

Virginia nodded. "It's like she put a fence around the children; anyone who tries to sell drugs to minors dies a tragic death."

"She didn't seem to have much use for Trooper Benson," Wren said.

Virginia shrugged. "He's not my favorite either."

"He's overzealous at times, but I've never had a negative experience with him," Samuel said.

"You sound like a local, Wren: you understand our local bigwig drug dealer," Dana Grace said.

After they finished eating, Dana Grace said, "Wren and I would like to go to the campground to salvage what we can. It will be drier than when Wren went this morning, so we may be able to get close to our trailers to load everything we can salvage."

"I'd like to go, but if you can do without me, I'd like to catch myself a nap," Samuel said.

"My truck or your truck, Wren?"

"Unless you need to indoctrinate your truck to campground mud, my truck's been mudded."

"Good point; there's no reason to clean two trucks tomorrow."

"I am totally fascinated by the logic of you two," Samuel said, "which means I still don't understand girls."

On the way to the campground, Wren told Dana Grace about the conversation with her publisher.

Dana Grace asked, "If you quit, won't it be hard to find another job?"

"I've been writing freelance since I graduated from college; I keep enough in my savings for three months of expenses, but I almost always pick up something interesting within a week or so."

"That is so outside my realm of understanding." Dana Grace shook her head.

"That was how I felt at first after college when all I could get was freelance work, but I came to enjoy the feeling of being my own boss. I'm pretty sure I'm not office material."

Dana Grace chuckled. "You'd be fine if Rascal's desk was next to yours, except he'd be off socializing."

"You're right; Rascal's not office material either."

When they arrived at the campground, Wren's eyes widened as Dana Grace pointed toward the restrooms and the trail. "Look at all the state police cars; something's going on."

Wren slowed to a crawl as she weaved around the trucks and cars that were randomly parked in the middle of the roadway as other campers removed items from their trailers and RVs.

"I'll park as close as I can to your trailer, Dana Grace; I don't have much left in my camper except what's in the overhead cabinets and my kitchen things. I'll come help you after I empty my trailer."

Rascal waited outside while Wren stuffed her towels and a set of sheets into her duffel bag that was in an overhead compartment. After she emptied the overhead compartments, her duffel bag was still only half full.

She carried it to the outside kitchen and added her pots, a pan, and her utensils. *A box would have been more convenient for the kitchen things.* "I guess that's about it, except I'd like to check my camping chairs; maybe I can salvage them if I scrub them."

After she tossed her duffel bag into the truck bed, she hurried back to her camper, and Rascal followed her. When she opened the compartment where the camping chairs were stored, she stuck her head inside the compartment and sniffed. "Doesn't smell moldy or stinky." She pulled out her wet chairs and carried them to her truck.

Wren returned to her camper; while Rascal waited, she went inside. "I won't be long. I'll make sure I'm not leaving behind anything I want."

Her phone rang.

When she answered, the sheriff asked, "Where are you?"

"I'm at the campground. Dana Grace and I are salvaging what we can from our campers."

"Does anyone know about the pouch?"

"Only you and Greta," Wren said.

"Keep it that way. I'll be at Apple Jack's Orchard with Samuel Hudson later. He'll let Dana Grace know to meet him there."

When Wren and Rascal reached Dana Grace, she was in conversation with another camper.

The man glanced at Rascal. "Well, I better get going; I've got a long night ahead of me since I'm driving straight through to St. Louis, Missouri."

The man strode to his truck then headed toward the exit.

Wren lowered the tailgate then followed Dana Grace to her trailer. Dana Grace handed a suitcase to Wren. "I think Rascal scared him away. Good boy, Rascal. The man was okay for a while, but he was making me uncomfortable right before you showed up. I do know why the state police are here, though. One of the campers that was one of the first to come here to empty his trailer found a man who had drowned in Bootleggers Creek, so the crime scene investigators are here. No one knows who the deceased was yet."

Wren slid the suitcase into the back of the truck then returned to the trailer door; Dana Grace handed her a plastic bin then followed Wren with another bin in her arms.

"That's it," Dana Grace said. "I wonder if the restrooms are open."

"If you want to check, Rascal and I will stay here with our things."

Dana Grace glanced around. "Good idea; there are a lot of people here that I don't recognize."

Before she stepped away, Dana Grace whispered, "Do you carry, Wren?"

Wren nodded.

"Good; so do I." Dana Grace hurried to the restrooms.

Wren stared at a muscular, middle-aged man two rows away as he furtively surveyed his surrounding while he carried a large cargo box from a trailer. *That's Philip; I thought Hank said he lived in Chattanooga.*

While she stood next to the bed of her pickup, Ghost joined her. "It was that man what lived in Grandpap's house. That your friend?" He motioned with his head.

Wren glanced toward the restrooms. Dana Grace hurried away from the restrooms.

"Yes, she is."

Trooper Benson smiled as he approached Dana Grace.

"She doesn't like him much, does she? She's smart," Ghost said.

Wren raised her eyebrows as Philip headed toward her with a scowl; he glanced at Dana Grace and Trooper Benson then stared at Wren before he returned to his trailer.

Dana Grace smiled, nodded, and spoke to Trooper Benson briefly, but continued to hurry to her trailer.

"Don't let him catch you alone." Ghost disappeared.

Doesn't sound like Ghost has much use for Trooper Benson either.

Chapter Eleven

"We have to get out of here," Dana Grace hissed. "I'm getting spooked by everyone, including one of the most highly respected state troopers in our area."

Ghost would agree with you about being spooked. Wren snickered then glanced at Dana Grace. *Good; I didn't say that out loud or get caught making a bad joke.*

"I agree with you." Wren opened the back door for Rascal.

As Wren slowly drove her pickup through the crowd that was becoming agitated by the stress and the chaos, Dana Grace's phone rang.

"Hi, Uncle Samuel."

Dana Grace grimaced as a man shoved another man against a trailer. "We're leaving the campground right now, so we'll be there as soon as we can."

After Dana Grace hung up, she said, "It's really getting ugly here, isn't it?" She cringed and jerked away from her door as an angry man pounded his fist against the side of Wren's truck.

"Hang on." Wren turned sharply and careened through the empty sites to the exit then sped to the road and headed toward the Hudsons' house.

"That was impressive." Dana Grace glanced back at the campground. "I'm glad to be out of there. Uncle Samuel needs some help with the tour bus; it has to be cleaned before tomorrow morning."

On the way, Wren's phone buzzed a text. She handed her phone to Dana Grace. "Who is it from?"

Dana Grace peered at Wren's phone. "It's from Lorinda; she wants to know if you're okay."

"Reply for me and tell her yes, and I'm staying at the Hudsons'."

After Dana Grace responded, she said, "Lorinda said that Estelle is staying with her until Chester returns from Chattanooga."

"That's good."

Dana Grace glanced at Wren. "Why? Estelle is a major pain."

Wren smiled. "Not if you tell her how great the campground looks; she takes great pride in her work. Tell Lorinda, good."

"Takes all kinds," Dana Grace muttered as she sent the text.

"I told Aunt Virginia that Justin might come here," Wren said.

"That's exciting; when will he be here?"

"He isn't; I just made that up."

"Oh, you were asking for me; that was pretty slick." Dana Grace chuckled. "What did she say?"

"There's no waiting period for a marriage license in Tennessee."

Dana Grace snort-laughed. "Love it."

"I told her we weren't quite ready yet, but Justin was a law officer and wouldn't want anyone to know he was here. She said there aren't any neighbors that would drop by or see him, so he could be incognito."

"Wow. There's my answer; I'll let Max know we have a home base, then I'll talk to Aunt Virginia."

Dana Grace smiled as she sent a text. "Thank you so much, Wren, but I'm kind of sorry that Justin won't be coming here; I'll bet he would if you asked him."

Wren furrowed her brow. "I hadn't thought about that, but you're probably right, and I'd love it. You're a bad influence, Dana Grace."

Dana Grace giggled. "Thank you."

Samuel stood on the porch with the sheriff when they arrived at the gift shop. After Wren parked next to Samuel's truck, Dana Grace climbed out of the truck while Wren opened the back door for Rascal.

"The bus is in the garage; I loaded the UTV with some cleaning supplies. It won't take the two of us very long to clean it."

"Thanks for the help, Samuel; I'll see you tomorrow," the sheriff said as Samuel and Dana Grace left in the UTV.

"Let's sit on the porch, Wren; let me have the pouch, then I want to hear everything."

While Rascal prowled the grounds in front of the gift shop, Wren gave Sheriff Morgan the purple velvet pouch; he glanced inside then peered at Wren. "Are these her car keys?"

She nodded then told him about the flat tire, the boxes, the pouch and keys, and Trooper Benson.

The sheriff narrowed his eyes. "She gave you the pouch after Trooper Benson arrived?"

"Right; she told me not to let him see it and motioned for me to leave."

The sheriff nodded. "Trooper Benson took her to the Copper Kettle Diner and paid for a meal for her and left. She borrowed a man's phone and asked someone to pick her up at the back of the Copper Kettle then walked out through the kitchen. Nobody thought anything of it because Greta does odd things all the time, except the man whose phone she borrowed called me to tell me she had called a private number. I think he was disappointed he couldn't tell who she called and thought I might tell him or find out for him."

Wren smiled. "We amateur sleuths hate to run into a wall."

The sheriff chuckled. "That's life in a small town. I got another call from the Copper Kettle thirty minutes later; Trooper Benson had returned and was highly agitated that Greta was gone, and no one had noticed when she'd left."

"Trooper Benson's not very popular, is he?"

"He's too intense for some folks."

"You sound like Marshal Lewis when he's on duty."

"I'll take that as a compliment; he's a fine young man. I appreciated your call because I impounded Greta's car and had the operator tow it to the compound behind the sheriff's department."

"Do you think Greta knew you'd intercept the tow?" Wren asked.

"I think she counted on you calling me right away, so I could." The sheriff narrowed his eyes. "How much contact have you had with Trooper Benson?"

Wren told him about finding the Texas Tech man and Trooper Benson being the first to arrive; seeing him in the library parking lot after the podcast when he asked if she was an investigator; and Trooper Benson being at the campground with the investigating team after she and Dana Grace had finished loading salvageable items into her pickup.

"He didn't approach you?"

"As soon as Dana Grace joined me at the truck, she said she felt nervous about being at the campground, and even Trooper Benson made her uneasy, so we left immediately."

Sheriff Morgan peered at Wren. "She didn't mention what Benson said to her?"

"No, and I didn't ask; I noticed the overall tension was rising, so it made sense to leave."

"Did you have any problems leaving? I understand it got rough there."

"I drove slowly past the shoving that had broken out, but when a man slammed the side of my truck with his fist, I made a sharp turn toward the exit and slammed on the accelerator."

The sheriff stared at her. "That was fast thinking; they didn't have a chance to swarm your truck, which is probably what would have happened next."

Wren shuddered. "My only thought was to tell Dana Grace to hang on."

"You have good instincts, and you're smart enough to trust them. The crime scene investigators called for help when they realized the campground had become a full-blown brawl, but I'm glad you weren't caught in it." The sheriff rose. "Stay close to Samuel, and you'll be safe."

As the sheriff strode to his cruiser, Wren's phone buzzed a text from Betsy. "Call when you have time or ASAP."

Wren snickered. *Only Betsy would send a text like that.*

Betsy answered on the first ring. "This was just too good to wait to tell you; you had to hear this right away. The school board is meeting first thing in the morning because Terry announced at the Watering Hole Diner that she would commit to teaching only three months because she couldn't find a decent place to live. I heard a teacher offered Terry a bedroom and kitchen privileges at her house, but Terry turned it down because she wouldn't have an en suite bathroom. That means like a private bath, doesn't it? I think Terry was trying to create a little drama or sympathy or something, but it's a wonder our cell service didn't go down because half the town immediately called all the school board members."

"That's certainly over the top, isn't it?"

"She definitely went on a tear about the whole housing thing. I don't have any other news, and if I did, nothing could beat the news about Terry; what's going on with you?"

Where do I start? Wren rolled her eyes. "I submitted my article to Charlie; he'll get back to me later today."

"Is he still pulling his old trick of blaming the editor?"

"He's trying to, but it's not working very well for him."

"I need you to go to the fourth haunted campground, so I know what its story is," Betsy said. "I've been trying to research haunted campgrounds, and I have several possibilities in case Charlie falls through."

Wren giggled. "We'll see whether the one he has selected is on your list."

"I found a really cool one in Kansas, but that's the wrong direction, isn't it?"

"I'm pretty sure Charlie's fourth one is close to the east coast because the theme of the articles is haunted campgrounds across America."

Wren listened as the UTV roared toward the gift shop.

"I'll let you know as soon as he tells me, so you can have bragging rights," Wren said.

Betsy chuckled. "Talk to you later."

Samuel dropped off Dana Grace. "I've got a couple of things to do, then I'll be home not long after you."

Samuel headed toward the equipment shed, and Rascal bounded from around the corner to join Wren and Dana Grace.

On the way to the house, Dana Grace said, "The bus wasn't all that dirty, which is why it didn't take us long, but it's gleaming now. It was obvious the sheriff came here to talk to you. Is it anything you can talk about?"

"Justin is a worry wart; he might have asked the sheriff to hover."

"I'd argue with Justin, except it was a little scary at the campground," Dana Grace said.

"I'm glad we got there as early as we did. It's not like I have anything that's worth much, but I think some looters showed up."

"That would definitely explain why the fights broke out."

After Wren parked at the Hudsons' house, Dana Grace said, "I don't remember where your publisher is. We have to celebrate five o'clock his time, but what time is that here?"

"He's in California, so that's eight o'clock our time."

As they went inside, Dana Grace said, "That's the perfect time for party animals that are in bed by ten."

"A party tonight? Are we celebrating Wren's publication? Did you hear from your publisher, Wren?" Virginia smiled.

Wren giggled. "Charlie will let me know where I'm going next by eight, or I'll send him my resignation."

"We need something special, like applejack jam thumb cookies with a shot glass of Tennessee moonshine followed by hot applejack cider," Virginia said. "You know, a melding of Arizona and Georgia."

Wren and Dana Grace laughed. "How is that a melding of Arizona and Georgia, Aunt Virginia?" Dana Grace asked.

"Applejack rules." Virginia tossed her head.

"No argument from us," Wren said.

Dana Grace added, "Because we're here for the party."

"We'll have chili in about an hour; it's Samuel's favorite."

"I'm going to relax in my room and write." Wren raised her eyebrows at Dana Grace, who nodded.

When Wren headed toward her room, Rascal flopped down next to the stove, and Virginia chuckled. Wren closed her door then set up her laptop, so she could write while she relaxed on the bed with her feet up.

While she wrote, her phone buzzed a text from Lorinda. "Call when you can chat."

Wren called Lorinda, who answered almost immediately.

"I heard all the campers at the campground were damaged by the floodwater. Were you able to salvage what you could?"

"Yes, I went to the campground earlier and picked up my clothes, kitchen pots, and dishes."

"That's good; the state police said looters showed up at the campground while the state police crime scene team was investigating..." Lorinda exhaled. "A camper found Chester, Estelle's husband, in the flooded creek after the storm, but Chester didn't drown; he had been shot. Estelle is terrified that the state troopers will think she killed him because Chester told her he was filing for divorce, but the trooper hinted that Chester may have been involved in an illicit drug operation. He asked Estelle a lot of questions and told her they had a search warrant to search the house. After he left, Estelle was furious; she said the troopers were wrong, and there was no reason to give people something to gossip about because they wouldn't find anything in her house. I'm absolutely sick about the entire thing."

"I'm sorry to hear about Chester; did the trooper mention anything about evidence, or was he just speculating?"

"He didn't mention any evidence, and we didn't ask."

"Maybe all this will clear up in a few hours after they complete their search; I'm certain Estelle's house is in perfect order," Wren said.

"You're right about her house." Lorinda sighed. "She's resting in her old room now. I told her she and I would rebuild the campground together, and she's already working on a plan to reopen as soon as possible."

"She'll be happy maintaining the landscaping and the buildings while you manage your guests."

"She will, won't she? Thank you; I needed to talk to someone who understood Estelle."

Wren exhaled after they hung up. *At least no one knows I was the one who discovered Chester's body.*

Wren resumed writing but stopped in the middle of a paragraph when Dana Grace tapped on her door then came into Wren's room.

"Aunt Virginia and I had a long talk, and everything is set for Max to come here. I sent him a text, so we'll see what he thinks. Are you at a stopping point? Aunt Virginia wants us to keep her company while she cooks."

When they went into the kitchen, Virginia said, "Samuel called me. The state police identified the body found at the campground as Chester Hudson. Samuel isn't sure what this means for his and Lorinda's plans to build the café after the campground is back in operation, but he'll wait for her to bring it up. I don't think Chester planned to stay around much longer anyway because I overheard him and Philip talking in the gas station about their business in Chattanooga."

"That might explain why Estelle seemed to be taking over more of the work around the campground," Dana Grace said.

Virginia said, "Wren, I want to hear more about your novel and how it's going."

Wren giggled. "That's a very dangerous request to make of a writer."

While Wren told her about Miss Miranda and her box of stories, Dana Grace excused herself when her phone rang.

After Dana Grace went into her room to answer her phone, Virginia said, "She's been anxiously waiting to hear from Max.

Thank you for giving me a little practice before she talked to me about him. I might not have reacted quite as calmly otherwise because I wouldn't have immediately understood why she hadn't mentioned earlier that she was married."

Wren exhaled. "I was worried about what you'd think."

"I still think you should tell Justin to come here." Virginia smiled.

"That is really tempting." Wren returned her smile.

Virginia glanced at the clock. "We have another hour and a half before we know which way the publishing wind blows. Speaking of publishing, what are your plans for your novel?"

"First, I want to finish it; after that, I'm not sure."

"Isn't it wonderful that you have options?"

Wren's phone rang, and she squealed, "It's Justin."

Virginia smiled; Wren answered while she hurried to her room.

"How are you doing?" he asked. "Have you heard anything from Charlie?"

"He loved the article just like he did the other two, but..."

Justin jumped in, "the editor."

"Exactly, except this time, he has until five o'clock his time to tell me whether he's publishing it and where my next assignment is, or I'll send him my resignation at five oh one."

"I can fly out tomorrow and be in Chattanooga by late tomorrow afternoon."

"What? Why would you want to fly here?"

"We'll pick up a fifth wheel in Chattanooga and head back to Hidden Gulch."

"I'm not sure..."

"I understand; it was a bad idea. Forget I brought it up."

"No, it's not a bad idea, and I'm not forgetting it. I was going to say I'm not sure you can get a flight out tomorrow. It might be a few days later, but if Charlie comes through, it will only be another week or two before I'm on my way back to Hidden Gulch. I would really like to write the fourth article, but it's all up to Charlie now."

"But if you resign, I'll fly to Chattanooga, and you'll pick me up, and we'll go shopping for a fifth wheel."

"I liked the one in the video," Wren said.

"I thought it would be perfect for you, me, and Rascal. How was your day?"

"Dana Grace and I salvaged what we could from our trailers, and I learned the man I found in the creek was the campground owner's son-in-law. Did you tell Sheriff Morgan to hover?"

"I never used the word 'hover'," Justin said.

"That's nice, so what did you say?"

"I told him you couldn't be trusted because you attracted killers like a porch light attracts moths."

"You did not."

"Maybe not, but doesn't that sound right to you?"

Rascal yipped.

"I think Samuel just came inside; we'll be eating soon; I have more to tell you, but I'll call you at eight Tennessee time."

"You still owe me another selfie," Justin said.

"I do not, but you owe me an I'm sorry kiss."

Justin chuckled. "I love you, sweetheart."

Wren sighed. "Love you too."

After they hung up, Wren hurried to the kitchen.

"You just missed Samuel; he and Rascal went for a walk," Virginia said.

"What can I do to help?"

"You can set the table with large bowls, spoons, and butter knives. I made cornbread to go with our chili."

While Wren set the table, she said, "When I was growing up, both Mom and Dad worked long hours, so Mom and Dad took turns ordering home delivery meals from our local restaurants. You make cooking look easy."

"I can give you some recipes that are perfect for beginners," Virginia said.

"That would be great; I think I'm losing my taste for fast food."

Dana Grace strolled into the kitchen. "Max will be here in three or four days; he'll let me know as soon as he can."

"That's great news; we'll plan another party to celebrate our nonexistent guest," Virginia said. "Wren, our supper is almost ready; do you mind chasing down Samuel and Rascal?"

"Not at all." Wren threw on her jacket.

As she left, Virginia said, "Dana Grace, should we find another quilt for your room? The flowered quilt seems a little frilly."

Wren zipped up her jacket against the cooler night air. As she walked toward the equipment shed, her phone rang; she frowned. I don't recognize the number, but it has a Tennessee area code. She shrugged and answered it.

"I wasn't sure if you'd answer or not," Greta said. "I wanted to thank you for moving so fast on my behalf. We didn't realize how close my cover was to being blown, which would have resulted in my untimely demise."

"Your cover?"

"I've been in the undercover business for almost forty years and been dang good at it, but I'm officially retired and have turned over my findings in the Dearheart investigation to the younger crowd. We still don't know who the killer is, but I'm convinced you have him spooked. Be careful, sweet girl. A frightened killer is likely to make careless mistakes, but that doesn't make him any less dangerous. I sure wish I knew who he was; I've had the feeling that I knew him, but his face was blurred, and the memory of his name disappeared into shadows. All I remember for sure is that they call him the boss. It would have been a triumphant finale for my long, never glamorous career if I'd taken him down, but it didn't work that way. I just realized I've been assuming the boss was a man even though I have no reason to support it; I suppose the boss could be a woman, except my gut tells me no. You've got the sheriff, Samuel, and Samuel's family; don't trust anybody else."

Greta hung up, and Wren stared at her phone.

Samuel and Rascal joined her.

"We saw you headed our way and thought we'd join you. Did you get a call from Justin?"

Wren smiled. "That was an old friend; I talked to Justin earlier. I'm the messenger: supper's almost ready."

"It's been great having you and Rascal here, Wren; I've enjoyed our walks," Samuel said. "Virginia's tickled that Dana Grace told her about Max. We heard about their secret marriage the day after they got married, so we've been biding our time until we were told officially."

Wren stared at him. "Really?"

"There aren't many secrets in our family. It's how most families are, isn't it?"

Wren snorted. "I thought it was just mine."

Samuel laughed. "It's another one of those life lessons."

As they neared the house, the cicadas buzzed, then another swarm joined in and were soon followed by a third chorus in a round robin of loud buzzing.

"Guess we're getting rain tonight, not that we need it," Samuel said as they went into the house.

When they went inside, Wren inhaled the tantalizing aroma of chili and its spices that swirled throughout the kitchen.

"The kitchen smells wonderful, honey," Samuel said.

Chapter Twelve

Virginia dished up the chili into the large bowls while Dana Grace put the cornbread on the table for everyone to serve themselves. Wren poured four glasses of sweet tea while Samuel fed Rascal.

As they ate, Samuel said, "I think we're going to get more rain tonight."

"I thought we didn't have any rain in the forecast before next week," Virginia said.

Samuel shrugged. "I'm going to make sure everything is put away, just in case."

"We need to empty the back of my truck, Dana Grace," Wren said.

"I didn't expect rain and thought it could wait until morning; so, I guess our plans changed."

"I'm glad you'll have something to do besides watching the clock. Wren, do you think your publisher will call, text, or send you an email?" Virginia asked.

"No telling. It depends on how he feels."

"How brave he is, you mean," Samuel said.

Wren nodded. "He definitely avoids any confrontation, if it's at all possible."

Wren backed her truck close to the back door, so it would be easier to empty the truck bed. Dana Grace hopped into the back of the truck and shifted all the items close to the tailgate, then they carried in their belongings and put them into their rooms.

After their fourth and last trip out to the truck, Wren said, "Didn't we load the truck in like two minutes?"

Dana Grace chuckled. "I guess panic does have its advantages."

Wren frowned at the box she was carrying. "I'll go through my things tomorrow to organize them."

Dana Grace nodded. "I'll need to do that too. I don't even remember what is in my bins, but at least I'm comfortable that I didn't leave anything behind."

As they walked in with the boxes, Samuel's phone buzzed a text.

Samuel pulled out his phone from the top pocket of his jacket. After he read it, he said, "Honey, the county animal services officer has two pups that were found alongside the road, and the shelter is overloaded. He's asking if we'd foster them."

"That's up to you; I'm fine with it," Virginia said.

Samuel sent his response. "I told him I'd meet him at the animal shelter in a half hour."

Rascal whined.

"Can we go along?" Wren asked.

Samuel read his latest text. "Sure can. The officer said they've been washed, and the vet checked them for fleas, ticks, and parasites, and they're fine."

Wren hurried to put her box in her room when her phone buzzed a text from Charlie.

She sighed as she read it. "Call me."

Wren returned to the kitchen. "I have to call my publisher; I don't know if it will be a short or long call, so I guess we can't go."

Rascal whined and gazed at Wren with his saddest eyes. Wren glanced at Samuel, whose expression matched Rascal's.

She rolled her eyes. "Of course, there's no reason Rascal couldn't go."

Samuel and Rascal beamed as they rushed out the door.

Virginia laughed after they were gone. "You folded there, Wren."

"Sure did, girlfriend." Dana Grace grinned.

Wren shook her head. "Their faces were so pitiful; I couldn't take the pressure."

"Do you want some hot cider to fortify you on your call? I have the church lady's special, which is very tame, then I have what Samuel calls the bootlegger's special."

"I think I'll start with the church lady's special and shift to the bootlegger's special if I hang up on Charlie."

After Virginia warmed the apple cider for the three of them, Wren called Charlie while Virginia and Dana Grace sat at the table with her.

"We're here for moral support," Dana Grace said.

"Plus, we're nosy," Virginia added.

"Works either way. Here goes nothing." Wren called Charlie. Charlie answered immediately.

"Did you find an editor for the Bootleggers Creek article?"

"An editor? Right, an editor to edit." Charlie cleared his throat. "I'll give you the good news first. Your article is excellent, and there was no logical reason to delay its release; I've sent it to the magazine printer for formatting and to the web developer who will add your article to the online magazine first thing tomorrow morning."

"What about Blake?"

"He said he'd read it after he gets back from vacation."

"How will that work? What if there's something he doesn't like about my article?"

"It will be published before he returns."

"He's not pulling his weight, is he?"

Charlie sighed. "Maybe he'll find something that suits him better."

"I hope so, for your sake, Charlie; this must be rough on you."

"Thanks, Wren. My other news isn't so great, but I'm hoping you'll understand."

Charlie exhaled then continued, "The manager at the RV dealership in Waco called the CEO and explained that he fully expects the insurance company to declare your camper a total loss. Your next campground assignment was almost nine hundred miles away from where you are; our original plan was for you to travel in your camper for the first two days then pick up your next RV. The CEO told me we have to come up with a new plan because it will be almost impossible to find hotels where Rascal can stay, and we can't expect you to sleep in your truck for three nights while you travel to the next campground for your last article."

"I'm grateful that the CEO recognized that," Wren said.

"He's an amazing guy; he knows his product, and he knows his customers."

"So, what are you thinking?" Wren asked.

"The CEO and I plan to discuss our options in the morning. He challenged me to come up with at least three campgrounds that were better than the one I'd originally picked to be your fourth assignment."

Wren smiled. "He went for the throat, didn't he?"

"He certainly did; so, do you have somewhere you and Rascal can stay in or near Dearheart for an extra day or two? Can you give me until the end of the day on Tuesday or hopefully Wednesday at the latest to let you know where your next assignment is?"

"One of the other campers has relatives in the area, and we're staying with them; they've already made it clear that we're welcome to stay a few extra days. Just keep me updated and let me know if you need more time."

Wren smiled as Virginia and Dana Grace high-fived.

"Thanks, Wren. I'm glad that you and Rascal have a safe place to stay." Charlie exhaled. "Now I'm under pressure to find some haunted campgrounds that are more interesting than the one I'd planned." Charlie hung up.

Wren raised her eyebrows. "He hung up on me."

"We didn't plan on that, did we? I love that you'll be staying longer, but he still sounded stressed from what I could hear," Virginia said.

"He did, didn't he?" Wren said.

"You don't sound like you think he was being sincere," Dana Grace said.

"I think Charlie thrives on stress," Wren said.

"It was nice of you to be so sympathetic." Virginia rolled her eyes.

Wren giggled. "Charlie and I have the same level of sincerity, but in this case, I think he was trying."

"So, what is he stressed about?" Virginia asked.

"The CEO told him to find three haunted campgrounds that were more interesting than the one he had originally planned."

"Ooo, that CEO is wicked," Dana Grace said. "We like him."

"I have to call Justin." Wren hurried to her room.

"Talk loud, so we don't have to strain our ears," Dana Grace called out.

Wren sat on her bed and called Justin.

"You're calling early; do you have good news or bad news?" Justin answered before the second ring began.

Wren snorted. "That's a judgment call. My article will be published online tomorrow morning and be included in the next print issue of the magazine."

"That's a surprise; I didn't expect the editor to approve your article since he was so balky about the previous two."

"I think he's lost interest and is trying to find another job."

"What will that mean for the magazine?"

"Charlie has connections; he'll find a decent editor," Wren said.

"What about your camper and your next assignment?"

"The assignment Charlie had planned for me won't work because it would take three days to get there, and Rascal and I can't travel that far without the camper. The CEO told Charlie to come up with three more haunted campgrounds that are closer and more interesting."

Justin chuckled. "The CEO must have a particular style of camper he wants you to evaluate. Did Charlie give you a timeframe?"

"He said Wednesday at the latest."

Justin sighed. "Too bad he didn't say a week. You could fly here then fly back at the end of the week. How quick can you get Rascal certified as a service dog?"

"If I flew there, I'm not sure I'd want to fly back."

"Works for me, so what's the downside other than your friends and readers will be disappointed?"

Wren snorted. "I think they'd be more irate than disappointed. Can you imagine the grief we'd get from Betsy and Socorro?"

"More than I get now because you haven't started the fourth article? According to Betsy, I need to speed up the process."

"Charlie didn't tell me where the original haunted campground was, but if it was almost nine hundred miles from here, I'd be that much farther from Hidden Gulch, so the few days of delay might not be all bad."

"Hi, honey, we're home," Samuel called out as he came in the back door.

Rascal burst into her bedroom followed by two six-month-old beagle puppies.

Wren giggled. "Rascal and Samuel just returned from the animal shelter with two beagle puppies that Samuel and Virginia are going to foster while the animal shelter tries to find their owners. I'll talk to you later; I love you."

"Send me a picture of the pups; I love you too, sweetheart."

Wren hurried to the kitchen followed by Rascal and the two scrambling puppies.

"What are their names?" Wren asked.

"We don't know," Samuel said. "The animal service officer said we could name them, and they'd learn their names in a few days."

"Won't they be confused when we find their owner?"

Dana Grace picked up her phone. "I'll check." She scrolled then said, "This says they'll recognize their original owner and their names."

"The little girl isn't spayed, but the boy pup is neutered; neither one of them is chipped, and they are from the same litter and are healthy in spite of how underweight they are. The vet said they were housebroken because they whined to go outside. He guessed they've been on their own for a while, so they didn't get separated from their owner by the flood."

Virginia knelt next to the puppies and rubbed their bellies. "Okay, pups, what are your names?"

Samuel cleared his throat. "Rascal and I had a chat on the way home. The boy is Jack, and the girl is Brandy."

Virginia laughed. "You and Rascal named them? Those are absolutely perfect names."

Rascal yipped then grinned.

Samuel smiled. "I have their crates with their blankets and their food from the shelter in the back of my truck."

When Samuel headed to the back door, Rascal yipped then he and the puppies followed Samuel.

"We'll help." Dana Grace and Wren followed Samuel and the dogs.

After they'd brought everything inside, Samuel said, "I thought we'd keep their crates in the kitchen, so they'll be around people and can go into them anytime they want."

"If we shift the cabinet a few feet, both crates can be under the window and close to the back door," Virginia said.

When the kitchen cabinet and table were rearranged to Virginia's satisfaction, Jack and Brandy sniffed the crates then went inside first one then the other. After Jack came out of the crate and returned to the other one, Brandy pawed her blanket into a pile while Jack watched her intently. When she flopped down on her blanket, Jack rearranged his blanket then laid down on it as he faced Brandy.

"Do we close the doors?" Virginia asked.

"It's probably what they are used to," Samuel said.

When Samuel latched the crates closed, Jack and Brandy closed their eyes.

Rascal laid down in front of the crates as Virginia turned on the hall light.

"I'm ready for bed too," Wren said.

"Right behind you," Dana Grace said.

After Samuel turned off all the lights in the kitchen, Virginia asked, "Aren't you leaving a night light on for the puppies?"

"They'll be fine with Rascal," Samuel said.

Wren changed to her pajamas and climbed into bed. She punched her pillow to fluff it the way she liked it then smiled. *Brandy would approve.*

She closed her eyes. *I wonder what Justin is doing.*

When her phone buzzed a text, she grabbed it off the nightstand. *Justin.*

"Call?"

He answered her call immediately. "Are you busy?" he asked.

"I just climbed into bed."

"Good; we can talk."

"About what? Is there something we need to talk about?"

"Yes, we need to talk about anything and everything. I want to be with you when you fall asleep."

Wren giggled. "The puppies are beagles; the animal service officer said they are brother and sister. Mr. Hudson said he and Rascal named them Jack and Brandy."

Justin chuckled. "I'll bet Rascal's with them, isn't he?"

"Of course. He's already working on their training."

"Do we want to get puppies for Rascal to train after you return to Hidden Gulch?"

"I don't think so; he enjoys training puppies, but if they were with us all the time, he'd never get any time off."

"Ouch. I'd hate that; it would be like making him the marshal of a small town or a talented journalist who solves murders, wouldn't it?"

Wren snort-laughed then covered her mouth. "You're going to make me wake everyone up."

Chapter Thirteen

When Wren woke the next morning, her phone was on her pillow with her face on top of it.

She giggled. "I fell asleep on the phone, literally."

"What? What did you say?" Justin's voice was groggy.

Wren's eyes widened. "You're still on the phone? We both fell asleep?"

"Our first night sleeping together," Justin said.

Wren hissed, "I can hear your smirk, Marshal Lewis; it's most unbecoming."

"You are absolutely gorgeous in the morning; did you know that?" Justin yawned.

Virginia's voice drifted from the kitchen. "Coffee's ready, honey. I'll pour you a cup to take with you when you and the puppers go outside."

"The folks are in the kitchen," Wren whispered. "We're gonna get caught."

Justin laughed. "Love it; thank you for sleeping with me."

"Justin!" Wren's voice was louder than she meant it to be.

"If Justin's in your room, tell him the coffee's ready," Virginia said.

Wren whispered, "Virginia said to tell you the coffee's ready. She's got remarkable hearing."

Justin chuckled. "Go get your coffee and make up a good story. I love you, sweetheart."

"I love you too, even if you are a terrible tease."

After they hung up, Wren hurried to the kitchen.

"So, what's the scoop? Why were you yelling at Justin?" Virginia asked.

"Bribe me with coffee, and I'll tell all."

Virginia poured a cup for Wren then refilled her cup before she sat at the table and raised her eyebrows expectantly.

After Wren told her about falling asleep while she and Justin were on the phone and waking up with him still there, Virginia asked, "He said something absolutely outrageous, didn't he?"

Virginia sipped her coffee.

Wren rolled her eyes. "He said 'thank you for sleeping with me.'"

Virginia spewed her coffee and coughed.

"I'm so sorry." Wren jumped to grab the paper towels.

Virginia laughed until tears ran down her face while Wren handed her a paper towel. "Don't be sorry; it was my fault thinking it would be tame. He is good with the zingers, isn't he?"

"I kind of started it because I told him the folks were in the kitchen, and we were going to get caught."

"Oh, my goodness, as early as it is in Arizona, and he was right in step with you? You absolutely must marry that man, especially since you've already slept with him." Virginia chortled.

Dana Grace yawned as she padded into the kitchen. "You slept with Justin? When was that? What did I miss?"

Wren glared at Virginia, who snort-laughed.

Wren sighed. "Coffee first, Dana Grace; you'll only enjoy the story if you're wide awake."

When Dana Grace wrapped her hands around her cup, Virginia asked, "Which version do you want? The lame Wren story, or my vividly awesome true story?"

"Lame for now, then the Virginia story later when I'm more awake and can enjoy the shocking side of Wren Weaver."

Dana Grace drank her coffee while Wren repeated her story about falling asleep then waking with Justin on the phone and what he said.

Dana Grace smiled. "That wasn't lame; it was hilarious. What's the Virginia story?"

Virginia poured herself another cup of coffee. "Samuel picked up Justin at the airport in Chattanooga late last night because Justin wanted to surprise Wren at breakfast this morning. We had no idea that he would sneak into her bedroom. Samuel gave him a time out; Justin will be in the barn for another thirty minutes."

Wren and Dana Grace laughed.

"Serves him right," Dana Grace sniffed.

"Serves who right?" Samuel asked as he and the dogs came inside.

"That's our cue to get dressed for breakfast; Aunt Virginia will explain." Dana Grace followed Wren out of the kitchen.

While she dressed, Wren smiled when Samuel roared with laughter.

After Wren and Dana Grace returned to the kitchen, Virginia scrambled eggs in her large cast iron skillet. Dana Grace made another pot of coffee while Wren set the table, and Samuel fed the dogs.

Virginia placed a loaf of sliced apple cinnamon nut bread and the large bowl of scrambled eggs on the table.

"I'd like to take Rascal to work with me this morning, so Jack and Brandy can get a little training," Samuel said. "Would you mind picking them up around lunchtime, so the pups can get their mama time with Virginia this afternoon, and Rascal can get a break?"

"That would be fine with me; what do you think, Rascal?"

Rascal yipped then smiled as Jack and Brandy copied his yip.

"Are you riding with us, Dana Grace?" Samuel asked.

"If you don't mind; I can't think of any reason I'd need my truck."

After everyone had eaten, Wren said, "Before you leave, I'm supposed to send Justin a picture of Brandy and Jack."

Jack and Brandy stared at Rascal who sat to pose for a photo. When he yipped, they sat on either side of him and smiled exactly like he did. Wren took two photos, then Samuel said, "Good job." He gave the dogs treats while they sat; when Rascal yipped, the two puppies yipped in response.

"I'll help with the dishes, so y'all can leave whenever you're ready," Wren said.

After they left, Virginia said, "I have errands to run this morning in town; you're welcome to go with me or stay here."

"I wouldn't mind having some writing time; I've gotten behind schedule," Wren said.

"Schedule?"

"It's self-imposed; I work better under deadlines."

"That makes sense for a journalist; if you couldn't work under a deadline, you'd be unemployed, wouldn't you?"

Wren set up her laptop on the kitchen table then drafted a quick list of major upcoming events for her novel.

Virginia stopped at the door with her keys in her hand. "Are you sure you'll be okay? You could go with me if you like; I'll be back before lunch."

"I thought I'd try something new and set a timer to do some sprints."

Wren took a stretch break after typing for two hours. She threw on her jacket and went outside. *I should go to the barn and tell Justin everyone has left, so he can come out of the barn.* She sighed. *Wouldn't it be great if he was there waiting for me?*

She strolled around the house. *No twinges or aches in my ankle.* She picked up her pace as she strode down the driveway. She examined the road and ditches. *Still wet, but not as bad as it was yesterday.*

When she strode toward the house, her phone rang.

Kendra said, "I had signed up for the online magazine and just received an email that it is published. I just wanted to be the first to tell you."

"I appreciate it; Charlie said he was going to publish it today, but it's nice to know that he really did."

"Are you doing okay? I heard there was a lot of flooding near you."

"The campground was flooded. Another camper and I evacuated before the rain hit and are staying with her relatives who live nearby."

"That's terrible; what about your camper?"

"It was ruined by the high water, and the insurance will probably declare it totaled. Charlie and the CEO for the RV manufacturer are discussing a change to my fourth campground because Rascal and I can't travel more than a day to pick up another camper."

"You could easily go to Chattanooga, couldn't you?"

"We could, but I think the CEO has a specific type of camper that he wants me to evaluate."

"That makes sense," Kendra said. "Are you enjoying your brief break from the world of magazine deadlines?"

"I really am; I'm making progress on my novel, and Rascal has two six-month-old beagle puppies to train."

Kendra chuckled. "I'll bet he's loving life."

"He is; Mr. Hudson brought the puppies home last night, and Rascal and the two beagles went with him to work at his apple orchard this morning."

"Our big news is that Tara is still our accountant; I hold my breath every day, but she and Gage seemed to be a little more relaxed around each other. We'll just have to see how it goes."

After they hung up, Wren strode to the house.

She sat at the table and opened her laptop. *I took the pictures of Rascal and the beagle puppies, but I forgot to send one to Justin.*

She opened her photos and smiled at them. *They're pretty much the same, but the second one is slightly cuter.* She sent the second one to Justin in a text.

She idly scrolled through her photos then came to the pictures she'd taken at the raceway concession stand; she furrowed her brow as she carefully examined each one. *Lorinda said the trooper thought Chester could have been involved in a drug operation.*

Wren texted the sheriff. "I have some photos I'd like to send to you."

The sheriff called her. "Whatcha got, Wren?"

"Rascal and I were exploring before the flood, and I took some photos of the old raceway concession stand for a future blog. I thought they had a small still set up for applejack, but it could be something else."

"How many do you have?"

"I don't know; less than ten, I think."

"Send away; if there's anything interesting, you don't mind if I send them on to the Crime Scene folks, do you?"

"Not at all."

The sheriff called her back a few minutes after she sent them.

"Who knows you have these?" Sheriff asked.

"Nobody."

"Keep it that way; I've been worried about a potential leak somewhere. If you don't mind, I'm going to claim that I took the photos, but I don't expect anyone to ask. I realize anyone who is tech savvy will know that's not true, but I'm hoping that's not the level of technical expertise our criminal has."

After they hung up, Wren exhaled then switched her focus to the next chapter of "High Falutin' Killer."

Two hours later, the sound of a car coming up the driveway interrupted Wren. She peered out the window then rushed to the back door to help Virginia with the groceries.

Virginia smiled as she parked then climbed out of her car. "I had a list, but I spotted items that were on sale, so my cart was overflowing by the time I got to the checkout line."

Wren carried in sacks of groceries while Virginia put them away.

"What took up most of my time, though, were all the people I ran into who wanted to talk about you. At least a dozen people told me they listened to Hank's podcast and signed up for the magazine. Did you know the magazine was published this morning with your articles?"

"I didn't know until I got a call about an hour ago from someone in Texas who had subscribed."

"Well, evidently, I'm your Tennessee contact because everyone in town knows you're staying with us. All the podcast listeners wanted to know when you'll publish your book. I told them you had to finish it first, and a couple of them are holding me personally responsible for announcing your publishing date. What do you know about publishing?"

"The biggest thing I know is that I've got a lot to learn."

"I hoped that was what you'd say, so I stopped by the library, and Lilibeth gave me three books to read on self-publishing. I'll let you know if they're worth reading. You write, and I'll vet the publishing side for you."

"You don't have to do that; it will be a lot of work."

"I've felt like I was getting stagnant; learning about publishing will flex my brain cells. While I was talking to

Lilibeth, Hank's sound engineer, Philip, came into the library. He said he saw my car and wanted to know if you were there with me. He asked me several questions about you, but they seemed more like ones that our nosy old ladies would ask, so I played ignorant."

"Really? Like what?"

"When were you leaving? Where were you going? Questions that weren't in line with the questions asked by everyone else like when was your book going to be published, or when was your next magazine article going to be online? I mentioned how odd I thought his questions were to Lilibeth, and she said engineers have strange thought processes that make no sense to the non-engineer. To be fair, though, he wasn't the only one who asked odd questions. One of our elderly ladies asked me if she knitted you a sweater, would I mail it to you. I can tell you it will be a dog sweater for a dachshund because that's all she knows how to knit; we'll donate your dachshund's sweater to the animal shelter on behalf of Rascal."

"He'd like that."

"What about you? Did you get any writing done?"

"The timed sprint helped me focus. After a break outside, I racked up more words."

"Good; I was worried that it would be too quiet for you."

Virginia's phone rang.

"Hi, honey."

Virginia glanced at Wren as she listened.

"I'll bring lunch, and we can picnic, then we'll bring back Rascal, Jack, and Brandy."

After she hung up, she said, "Samuel can't get away after all, and of course, Dana Grace can't leave the gift shop. Samuel asked if we could pick up the puppies because they were getting tired. I'll pack a quick lunch, but you heard that. Is it okay that I volunteered you?"

"Of course, my truck is perfect to pick up Rascal and the puppies."

"Give me a couple of minutes to make and pack sandwiches. Would you pull out water from the fridge and cookies from the freezer?"

When they were on the road to the orchard, Virginia said, "The orchard has a picnic area not too far behind the gift shop. Dana Grace can join us because we'll be able to see if anyone drives up. Monday's our slowest day, and it's rare for anyone to come to the orchard at lunchtime, but if we counted on no one showing up, we'd have a tour bus pull in, wouldn't we?"

Wren chuckled. "Do you get tour buses very often?"

"Several times a week, but they usually call unless the driver and their office get their signals crossed, which sometimes happens."

After Wren parked next to the gift shop, Virginia said, "If you'll tell Dana Grace we're here, I'll text Samuel to meet us at the picnic table."

When Wren went into the shop, Dana Grace smiled. "I knew Uncle Samuel would call for relief. The puppies have had a fantastic morning, but they've worn themselves out."

"Virginia packed a picnic lunch for all of us. We're supposed to meet them at the picnic area."

As they strolled around the building, Dana Grace said, "Uncle Samuel added the picnic area when I was a kid. Our customers love having a place to eat their lunch before they get back on the road."

While Virginia pulled out plates and food, Rascal trotted alongside Samuel as he pulled a wagon with the puppies riding inside.

"Poor babies; they are tired," Virginia said. "Well, we'll eat and run."

Virginia filled a water bowl from the nearby faucet then put it into the wagon for the puppies while Wren filled a second water bowl for Rascal.

While they ate, Samuel said, "John Andrew will be along shortly."

"I packed two sandwiches for him," Virginia said.

Wren's mouth opened as she stared at a young man who strode toward the picnic table. He wore a brown shirt and a brown ball cap over his shock of red hair; brown suspenders held up his blue jeans, and the laces on his scuffed work boots were frayed. *A young version of...*

"Ghost?" she muttered.

"Are you okay, Wren? You look a little pale," Dana Grace said.

Virginia waved. "Good to see you, John Andrew."

The teen smiled. "Uncle Samuel told me I'd better pick up my sandwiches before Jack and Brandy ate them; I told him he's the boss."

Wren realized her mouth was still open. She shook her head as she pressed her lips together. *He even sounds like Ghost.*

Jack opened his eyes when John Andrew said his name, and Brandy flipped her tail.

"They're biding their time until they think no one's watching." Virginia returned his smile then introduced Wren and John Andrew.

"I heard you on Mr. Hank's podcast, Miss Wren. That new book of yours sounded real interesting."

"Thank you, John Andrew."

"Miss Lilibeth told me the library would order it as soon as it was available; she already has a wait list."

"That's the magic of Hank's talent in podcasting."

"Sure is; it sounded like you, Hank, and I were sitting on a porch just chatting."

"That's a perfect description, John Andrew," Samuel said.

"Here are your sandwiches; are you going to join us?" Virginia asked.

"No, ma'am; I'd like to get back to work as quick as I can."

Virginia handed him a lunch sack. "That's what I expected you to say, so here are two sandwiches and a few cookies for you."

Samuel gave John Andrew a bottle of water before the teen returned to the orchard. "John Andrew has the same clear blue eyes that Miss Ruth Whitaker has." Wren said.

Virginia and Samuel side-glanced at each other.

"I've never noticed that before." Dana Grace narrowed her eyes as she glanced at Virginia and Samuel. "There's a story, isn't there?"

"I have to get back to work, so I don't look like a slacker, which I am, if you compare me to John Andrew." Samuel hopped into the UTV and headed toward the orchard.

"Clarence Whitaker had a sister who ran off with one of Norman Hudson's brothers; I'm not sure I ever knew their names, but after her husband died in the war, and I think it was World War I, the young woman came home with a baby. The Whitakers shunned her, but the Hudsons took her in and helped raise her son. I think she would be John Andrew's great-grandmother," Virginia said.

"I've never heard that story before," Dana Grace said.

"It's one of those old, scandalous stories that I heard from my grandmother; nobody cares anymore. It's interesting that you noticed a resemblance, Wren. I don't think I've ever noticed what color Miss Ruth's eyes are."

"What about John Andrew's red hair? Where did that come from?" Wren asked.

"His mother is a redhead, and there are several redheads on the Hudson family tree, so no one was surprised when John Andrew was born. Why do you ask?"

"Miss Ruth implied that red hair was a Whitaker characteristic when Lilibeth told her my hair had red streaks."

"That may or may not be true; Miss Ruth is one of the best storytellers, in every sense of the word, in east Tennessee, so she may have been creating a local persona for you."

Wren furrowed her brow. "Maybe that's why Hank referred to me as 'our own'."

"Being local opens a lot of doors around here; I'm sure that's what they were doing," Virginia said. "Hank is a remarkably astute marketer and having a local author on his podcast would definitely give his show a boost in ratings."

"I wouldn't have thought of that because marketing's not my strong suit," Wren said.

"If you get stumped by something, shoot a quick email to Hank; I'm certain he'd love to advise you."

Dana Grace said, "I want to hear more old family stories, Aunt Virginia."

"Most of the stories that folks considered shocking when I was a girl are actually really tame now, but I'll ask Lilibeth about an oral history day for storytellers. I'm sure other libraries have hosted them, but Lilibeth would know. An event like that might give a little boost to our community."

Dana Grace rose from the picnic table. "My lunch break is over; I hear a car coming up the drive. If I'm going to beat them into the gift shop, I better hustle. Thanks for lunch, Aunt Virginia." Dana Grace hurried to the gift shop.

"We've been abandoned; ready to take these pups home, Wren?" Virginia asked.

While Wren pulled the wagon with Brandy and Jack to her truck, Virginia cleared the picnic table. After Wren opened the door, Rascal hopped into the truck. She placed the exhausted puppies on the back seat.

When they were home, Virginia carried Jack while Wren carried Brandy into the house.

Jack and Brandy took turns taking long drinks from their water bowl, then Rascal nosed the door. After Wren opened it, the puppies trotted behind Rascal as he went outside.

Virginia shook her head. "I expected them to be too tired to go outside."

"I think puppies have two speeds: super-fast and collapse," Wren said.

"I think you're right; what's your plan for the rest of the day? Are you going to write?"

"I think I will, at least for a while. What about you?"

"I'm going to dive into one of the books Lilibeth gave me."

Chapter Fourteen

Wren stared at her laptop screen with her fingers poised to type. "I got nothing," she grumbled.

Virginia looked up from her book. "Walk away then."

Wren wrinkled her nose. "It's more than the novel; it's..."

Wren was interrupted by her phone ringing. "I don't know who this is, but it's a Texas area code."

Virginia rolled her eyes. "So, answer it."

When Wren answered, a man said, "Miss Weaver? Wren? I'm the manager from the dealership in Waco where you picked up your camper. The insurance company is overloaded with claims; they've asked if someone could send them some photos of your camper. I hate to ask, but is there any way you could do that safely?"

"I think so," Wren said.

"The claims adjuster sent me a list of three specific photos he needs and two additional ones, which are pictures of the camper in the campground, are what he called nice to have. Can I text it to you?"

"Go right ahead; I'll do what I can."

"That's all anyone can ask; call me if you have any questions. I hate to bother you, but I appreciate your help."

After Wren hung up, Virginia asked, "Didn't sound like you were talking to a friend; are you okay?"

"It was the manager at the RV dealership in Waco. The insurance adjustor needs some photos to process their claim. He's going to text me their list; I'll see what I can do."

Wren's phone buzzed a text. After she read it, she said, "They are requesting three pictures. The first two are simple: exterior and interior showing damage. This third one, VIN number on the tongue of the trailer, sounds like a sticker or something."

"I think you're right, but you could check with Justin because he would know, but maybe you should call him anyway because aren't these things the insurance adjuster is supposed to do?"

"I'll text him and tell him I have a nonurgent insurance question, so he won't drop everything to call me."

After Wren sent the text, her phone rang.

"Are you okay?" he asked when she answered.

"Why wouldn't I be okay?" Wren asked.

"I didn't know if you were trying to tell me something in code, but I couldn't figure it out."

Wren sighed then told him about the call from the manager at the Waco dealership.

"It's not usual, but it might help them determine their priorities for the adjusters if they are overloaded with claims."

"I don't mind; it's a short, pleasant drive; anything interesting going on at Hidden Gulch?"

"Just our usual, which is pretty tame when you aren't here. I've been asked to review some reports as part of a peer review, which might not sound exciting, but I always learn something when I participate in a review."

After they hung up, Wren said, "Justin said there's no reason I shouldn't take the photos, and the drive will do me good because I need to clear my head anyway."

"I have some books I need to return to the library, but I'll do that later this week, if Samuel can watch the puppies at the orchard while I run into town."

"I don't mind dropping off the books for you," Wren said. "It gives me an excuse to go into town; while I'm there, I can fill up the truck."

"Are you sure?" Virginia asked.

"Positive; I think I need a little road time to clear my head."

After Virginia gave Wren the three books to be returned, Wren put on her jacket; Rascal followed her to the truck.

As she pulled onto the highway, Wren said, "I've enjoyed the Hudsons' hospitality, but I'm antsy to be on the road and heading toward our next assignment."

She glanced at the napping Rascal in her rearview mirror and smiled. *He'd never admit the puppies wore him out.*

After Wren parked in front of her camper, she surveyed the vacant sites and the deep ruts in the mud that crisscrossed the campground. "Looks like my trailer and two others are the only ones that haven't been towed away yet. Bootleggers Creek looks like a ghost town, no offense intended."

She opened the camper door and coughed. "The camper's starting to get that moldy smell; I'm not going in."

She snapped a quick photo of the floor where it had already buckled then stepped back to get a good shot of the camper with the mud and leaves that delineated the level of the flood waters.

"Now, we hunt for the elusive VIN sticker. The manager said it is most likely on the front left corner on the roadside of the camper." Wren walked around the camper.

She raised her eyebrows. "It's right where he said; I don't know why I doubted him." She wiped it with the sleeve of her jacket then snapped the picture.

She examined her photos then texted them to the manager.

He replied immediately. "Got them. Thanks. The CEO said the company owes you one."

Wren smiled. "Rascal, the CEO and I are even because he told Charlie to come up with a better haunted campground that wasn't so far away for us to travel from Dearheart."

Before she climbed into the truck, Wren said, "Let's see if the raceway was flooded. It seems to me that it was at a little higher elevation."

Before they turned toward the trail, Wren said, "I wonder if the house flooded."

Rascal barked then pointed toward the camper.

When Wren glanced at the woods that led to Estelle's house, a motion between the trees caught her attention; she stared as a dark shadow wavered then blended into the trees.

"I guess you're right; that would be trespassing, wouldn't it, but don't we want to check…"

Wren was drowned out by the sound of roaring engines and squealing tires coming from the raceway.

She smiled as she followed Rascal to her truck. *There's my answer: all is well in the stock car world.*

Before Rascal hopped into the back seat, Wren wiped his paws with the old cloth she kept in the pouch on the back of the driver's seat. As she scraped off the mud from her boots, she said, "Thank you, Ghost."

His voice drifted from the direction of the trail. "You betcha, doll. Me and dog want you to be safe."

On the way to town, Wren said, "I think I was worried about Ghost and the racetrack; I'm glad everything is okay."

When she reached the outskirts of Dearheart, Wren furrowed her brow. After she parked at the library, she sent a text to Justin. "At the library. Got the VIN number. Ghost let me know he and the racetrack are okay."

Justin sent a reply. "You heard the cars racing? That's great; I knew you would worry about Ghost."

She texted. "Doesn't make any sense, does it?"

"Not a bit," he replied.

She called him; when he answered, she giggled. "Thank you for your support."

"Any time, honey; it's nice to hear you laugh."

"I'm trying to be calm while I wait to hear from Charlie, but I'm really restless." She sighed. "The manager at the dealership in Waco appreciated the pictures I sent him. He told me the CEO of the company owes me one."

"Sounds like their claim would have been given a low priority, since no one was left homeless or in a dangerous environment. Thanks to the Hudsons, that wasn't your situation at all."

"They're really kind-hearted people; since yesterday, they've made room in their home for their niece and four strays," Wren said.

Justin chuckled. "I'm sure they don't see it like that at all."

Wren sighed. "I should probably go into the library. I love you; I knew you'd understand about Ghost. Oh, wait. Did I tell you about John Andrew?"

"He's not another one of your boyfriends, is he?"

"I don't have any boyfriends," Wren snorted.

"Excuse me?"

Wren felt her face warm. "Maybe one."

"Ah ha! I knew it," Justin said. "You can gush about how wonderful he is later; tell me about John Andrew."

Wren rolled her eyes. "John Andrew just graduated from high school and is related to Samuel Hudson, but he's a young version of Ghost, and according to Dana Grace, John Andrew is a natural-born mechanic."

"Wow, so he's related to the Whitakers somewhere along the line."

"You're right; I'll tell you the story Virginia told me sometime."

"How did you ask? You couldn't just blurt out Ghost."

"Oh, but I did; I couldn't imagine why Ghost was at the apple orchard. I don't think anyone heard me except Dana Grace; she told me I looked pale. I brought up Miss Ruth Whitaker and her claim that I must be related to the Whitakers because of my red hair. I'll tell you the whole story when I tell you Virginia's story."

"You know, if I was right there with you, you wouldn't have to remember to tell me all these interesting tidbits. I love you, honey; take care of your library errand."

After they hung up, Wren scraped her feet on the mat outside the door and Rascal wiped his paws before they went into the library.

Lilibeth beamed as they strolled inside. "Were your ears burning earlier, Wren? Hank and I were talking about you this morning. He's getting requests to make you a regular guest. Hank has a friend who's a bigshot in broadcasting, and the two of them are mulling it over and will most likely come up with some type of scheme that will work for you too."

"I'll be interested in hearing their plan for a regular remote guest on the podcast." Wren put the books she'd brought on the desk. "Virginia gave me these to return."

Lilibeth's eyes widened as she glanced at the front door. "Your shoes are all muddy. I'm surprised to see you here on a Monday in the middle of the afternoon."

Wren turned to see who had come inside the library.

Philip rubbed his forehead in an unsuccessful attempt to hide his scowl as he removed his shoes then set them outside the door. "I left some of my tools here on Saturday, boss. I suppose the podcast room is locked," he grumbled.

"We always keep it locked." Lilibeth opened a drawer then set a key with a green ribbon attached to it on the counter. "Here's the key."

Philip snatched up the key. "Better not be any of my stuff missing," he muttered as he hurried to the hallway.

After he slammed the podcast room door, Lilibeth shook her head. "He sure can be cranky when things don't go his way."

Lilibeth pulled out three books from a bottom shelf under her desk. "I have some books for you to take to Virginia; is she going to be your publisher? She's very definitely doing a deep dive into the subject; the rest of the books are her usual true crime books. She'll be an excellent resource for you if you get stuck at a point in your plot."

"She's studying independent publishing, so she can advise me on where to start after my novel's finished. I didn't know she read true crime stories; maybe I'll borrow some of her books to get some ideas."

"It always helps to have someone to bounce off ideas, doesn't it? You can name your publishing company Dearheart Gulch Press or better yet, Forgotten Bootleggers Trail." Lilibeth furrowed her brow. "No, that should be the name of your next book."

"You've read the haunted campground articles." Wren smiled.

"You're a talented journalist, Wren, but your true genius erupted when you brought those legends to life for your readers. You have a storyteller's soul, which gives you the gift of seeing how unrelated events tie together; don't be afraid to lean into it."

Wren raised her eyebrows. "Are you telling me to walk away from the safe path?"

"That's one way to put it, or maybe I'm suggesting you should seriously consider a path that might be more whimsical."

Lilibeth's hazel eyes twinkled as she pulled down the red frames of her thick glasses to peer at Wren.

Wren met Lilibeth's gaze. "Either way…"

"Yes." Lilibeth smiled. "Adventuresome or unpredictable: either way, it's you."

Wren nodded as she picked up the books for Virginia then left the library with Rascal at her side. *Either way, it's me. Wonder what Justin would say? I'll have to remember to ask him.*

Before she turned on the ignition, Trooper Benson pulled into the parking lot and strode to her truck.

Wren sighed. *I suppose it would be rude if I ignored him.* She lowered her window.

"I thought that was you, Wren." He peered at the books on the passenger's seat. "I didn't know you were into true crime, but I suppose it makes sense. Don't you worry that the perpetrator will think you're studying him? Seems like a pretty dangerous move to me; I thought you were smarter than that."

Trooper Benson narrowed his eyes. "You'll live a lot longer if you mind your own business."

As he stepped back from her truck, he tapped the brim of his hat. "Have a nice day."

Wren stared at him as he returned to his cruiser and left the parking lot. "I was either just threatened, or Trooper Benson has the worst social skills in the state, Rascal. No self-respecting killer would be that blatant, would he? I need an expert opinion; do I ask Justin or the sheriff?"

She sent Justin a text. "I have a law enforcement question. Call?"

He responded, "Is it urgent?"

"Not at all."

"Give me 15 minutes."

"Let's stop by the gas station and top off the gas tank, Rascal."

Wren's phone rang as she turned at the gas station. She parked in front of the store and answered.

"You have my undivided attention; what's up, honey?"

She told him what Trooper Benson said.

"What was your impression?" Justin growled.

"He has the reputation of poor social skills; I'm not sure if his intent was to remind me to be cautious, threaten me, or warn me because he knows something, which makes me think he's somehow involved."

"I'm going to call the sheriff, so you don't have to. I'll let you know what he says, or he may beat me to it and contact you for more information."

"I didn't mean to give you extra work; I can call the sheriff."

"Word would get around if you did; if the sheriff initiates the contact, it could be about any of the current investigations and not raise any eyebrows."

"Thank you; I appreciate it."

"I plan to ask the sheriff if he thinks you're in any danger because if he does, I'll be on the next plane."

"You don't have to..."

Justin interrupted her. "Yes, I do; it's hard enough to be so far away from you, but if there's any trouble, I want to be alongside you."

Wren's eyes welled up at the intensity in his voice. "I think that's the way life is supposed to be, isn't it?"

Justin's voice softened. "Yes, we belong together."

Wren nodded as tears slid down her cheek. *I don't know if I still want to go to my last assignment.*

"Are you okay? You're awfully quiet."

"I'm a little tired and worried about how Rascal and I will get to our next assignment."

"If you don't like it, or if Charlie takes too long to get back to you, I'll come get you. Remember when I told you I was afraid you'd say we'd always be friends, and you said we'd always be friends?"

Wren watched as cars pulled up to the pumps or parked in front of the store. *It's more than that; I'm really tired of being away from you.*

"Because it's true," Wren said.

"I think I finally understand; you'll always be my best friend."

Wren nodded. "That and more." Her eyes widened. *I didn't mean to say that out loud.* "I'm sorry; I didn't mean..."

Justin interrupted her. "That's okay; I didn't take it wrong."

"What didn't you take wrong? I'm tired of not seeing you when we talk, so I can glare at you. I meant what I said, but I didn't mean to say it out loud." Wren giggled. "Did you just understand that? I didn't."

Justin chuckled. "I'll pretend to understand, then I'll misinterpret it. Will that work?"

Wren laughed. "This is exactly why we'll always be best friends."

"I want to call the sheriff; we'll talk later. I love you, sweetheart."

Wren sighed then pulled up to the only open pump that was at the far end of the parking lot. A large box truck pulled in at the pump next to her and blocked her view of the rest of the pumps and the parking. After she filled the pickup's tank, she climbed into her truck and headed toward the exit. As she turned onto the highway, she glanced toward the store and raised her eyebrows as she watched Samuel and Trooper Benson who were standing near the door and were laughing. They shook hands, then Trooper Benson went into the store while Samuel scanned the parking lot then hurried to his truck.

"What was that all about, do you suppose, Rascal?" Wren asked as she headed toward the Hudsons' home.

After she and Wren parked near the back door, Jack and Brandy rushed to the pickup. Virginia smiled as she joined them.

While Rascal led the puppies on a chase around the yard, Virginia said, "They slept most of the afternoon; puppies play hard then crash, don't they? Did you have a successful trip? How was the campground?"

"Most of the trailers are gone; the campground is a mess from the heavy-duty trucks that pulled the trailers and RVs out of the mud before they towed them away. I got the VIN number and the pictures for the RV dealership manager. I returned your books, and Lilibeth sent you more to read."

Virginia chuckled. "Lilibeth takes care of me."

As they strolled toward the house, Wren said, "Rascal and I stopped for fuel, and I saw Samuel. I don't think he saw me because I was leaving and just happened to catch a glimpse of him coming out of the store."

"He told me he had a few things to pick up in town for the orchard; he doesn't mind running those errands since Dana Grace is managing the store for him. He claims the orchard operation runs itself, but I know how hard he works," Virginia said.

"I think he was talking to Trooper Benson, but he might have just been coming out of the store at the same time that the trooper went in."

"They probably stopped to chat; Samuel and Ollie have been good friends for years; I don't think anyone else could have tolerated Ollie for as long as Samuel has. Samuel claims Ollie is a conscientious state trooper and works hard, but he has no filters and gets on my nerves."

Chapter Fifteen

Wren furrowed her brow. "Have you had a run-in with Trooper Benson, Virginia?"

"I wouldn't quite call it that, but he stays away from me."

"How did you do that?"

"I was wired, as they used to say. Remember when we talked about Greta earlier? What do you know about her?"

"She was actually the direct opposite of what her reputation was."

"Good; I don't have to dance around with words then. I talked to Greta, who arranged for me to wear a wire, so she could record the conversation. After she gave me a copy, I played it for him, and he tried to claim I'd edited it; I didn't laugh at him, but I did roll my eyes. I told him the techies could tell and asked him if he really wanted to go that route. Greta told me that's what he would say and gave me the words that shut him up."

"That fits with the Greta I know," Wren said. "What did he say to you, or is it inappropriate of me to ask?"

Virginia snorted. "Every word that comes out of his mouth is straight out of the misogynist handbook. His wife died of cancer a few years ago, and his loss seemed to obliterate the few social skills that he had. He's always been more of a man's man; there are very few women who can tolerate him. I suspect he's angry at women because his wife died, and the rest of us didn't, but that's his problem, not mine. I don't feel sorry for him at all; he needs help dealing with his grief, but that's not my concern. Do I sound harsh?"

"I think you sound healthy."

"I regret that I didn't push it, though. Samuel tells me that there's a part of him that is trying to reach out." Virginia sighed. "I don't know about that."

"It doesn't matter because it doesn't excuse his outrageous behavior," Wren said.

"That's it exactly. How do you know all this?"

"I spent three weeks in a recovering drug addicts' home for girls; it was eye opening to say the least. I was hired by the corporation that managed the home to give them a perspective from a resident's point of view; it's one of the hardest assignments I've ever had."

"Because you felt sorry for the girls?"

"No because there were so many jaded young women."

"I couldn't do that," Virginia said.

"I couldn't either; I was supposed to be there a month, but after three weeks, I convinced the corporation I had enough data to write up my findings for them, and an additional week wouldn't have changed anything."

"That's depressing; what's your favorite assignment?"

"I spent two weeks at a donkey rescue farm where they also rescued dogs. I was really sad when I had to leave."

Virginia smiled. "I can see that in you; is that where you and Rascal got together?"

"You're good; yes, it was. My mom said she and Dad were lucky I didn't come home with a couple of donkeys." Wren smiled.

"If you go back to Arizona, will you miss the variety of assignments?"

"Maybe, but adding fiction to my skills will keep me busy for quite a while."

Virginia's phone rang. "This is odd," she said.

After she answered, she listened for few moments then became pale as she dropped into her chair. "Where is he?"

Tears welled in her eyes.

"Thanks; I'm on my way."

Virginia ran to her bedroom and returned with her purse. "Wren, Samuel was medevacked to the trauma hospital in Chattanooga; the details are sketchy, but he stopped to help a disabled vehicle, and a distracted driver hit him."

Before Virginia reached the door, Wren asked, "Why did you say the call was odd?"

"It was a private number. Will you take care of the puppies? I don't know how long I'll be gone."

"Stop a minute; I want to call the sheriff's office."

"The man said I'd get a call soon with more details, but I'm not waiting because every minute counts..."

"Give me just one minute." Wren stepped between Virginia and the door as she called the sheriff.

"Get out of my way, Wren." Virginia's face was inches from Wren's.

"I'm calling the sheriff."

When the sheriff answered, Wren said, "Virginia just got a call that Samuel had been hit by a car and medevacked to Chattanooga. Do you know anything about that?"

"There haven't been any medevac flights in weeks. Hold on."

"Virginia, the sheriff said there haven't been any medevac flights in weeks. Please sit down."

"Are you making that up, Wren?" Virginia growled.

"Please, just sit down."

The sheriff said, "Is Virginia still there?"

"Yes."

"Don't let her leave."

"Virginia, the sheriff wants you to stay here," Wren said.

"Did you even call the sheriff? I don't understand what's wrong with you." Virginia reached out to push Wren out of her way.

Rascal growled a low, guttural sound and bared his teeth. The puppies whined as they positioned themselves between Wren and Virginia.

Wren braced herself. "I don't think the puppies want you to knock me down."

Virginia stared at the puppies then at her phone when it rang; her eyes widened as she answered. "Samuel? Are you okay?"

Wren's knees grew weak; she exhaled as she leaned against the door to keep from falling.

Virginia sat at the table. "I got a call that you'd been hurt."

"Wren? Are you there, Wren?" the sheriff asked.

"Yes, I'm here; Virginia's talking to Samuel. I thought she was going to deck me."

"She was probably thinking about it."

"Rascal thought she was going to; I think the puppies were planning to break my fall."

The sheriff chuckled. "At least you had a good support team. Wren, what tipped you off that the call was phony?'

"Virginia did. When her phone rang, she said it was odd because it was a private number."

"Somebody wanted you to be alone."

"I don't know about that; I think someone wanted Virginia distracted with worrying about Samuel; I don't think they expected her to leave alone."

"Why?"

"I think Virginia knows something but doesn't realize it."

"I'd tell you to stay out of it, Wren, but I have a feeling I'd be wasting my breath; instead, will you call or text me the second you have even a hint what it might be?"

"I'll try."

"Wren, I'm okay now; come sit down before you collapse," Virginia said.

Wren stumbled on her way to the table.

"I'm sorry I scared you. Can I get you anything? How about a cup of coffee or hot tea?" Virginia rubbed her forehead. "Samuel and Dana Grace will be home before long, and I haven't started my spaghetti sauce yet."

"I'm fine." Wren furrowed her brow. "I think I'm extra stressed because I don't trust Charlie. He told me he'd get back to me tomorrow or Wednesday at the latest, but I'm anxious to know if he's made any progress at all, or if he's going to call me on Wednesday with another stalling excuse."

"Call him; I'll just mind my own business, but you have to be on speakerphone."

Wren giggled as she called Charlie.

He answered immediately. "You must have ESP; the CEO of the RV company and I just finalized our plans. You can pick up your camper in Mobile, Alabama, then go from there to the Lost Pirate Campground near Sirens Beach, Florida. It's an old campground and needs some work, but I'm sure you'll find the history of the area to be very interesting. I'll send you the address of the RV dealer; they'll have your RV ready for you tomorrow after lunch."

"Give me a second to check the mileage to Mobile." Wren shook her finger at Virginia's phone.

Virginia grabbed her phone and opened a map. "Seven to eight hours with breaks," she whispered.

"It's an eight-hour drive; I can leave early Wednesday morning, so I can arrive by five o'clock."

"You can't leave tomorrow morning?"

"No; it' s getting late and will be dark soon. I'll have to pack my truck and plan my route."

"Wednesday is good. The RV dealership is close to a campground, so you can stay there overnight then continue to Sirens Beach, Florida. The CEO said it's an easy four to five-hour drive."

"That sounds perfect; I'll check in at the Lost Pirate Campground on Thursday."

"That's great; I'll change your reservation in Mobile for Wednesday night and at Lost Pirate Campground for two weeks beginning on Thursday. I'll warn the owner at the campground in Sirens Beach you'll probably have your article written before the second week begins."

After Wren hung up, she grinned. "I didn't have to threaten to quit; isn't that amazing?"

Virginia's smile was weak. "I hate to see you go, but I'm happy for you."

Wren texted Justin. "Next assignment: I leave on Wednesday for Mobile, Alabama, to pick up my camper then leave on Thursday for Lost Pirate Campground in Sirens Beach, Florida."

Justin replied, "Yay! Send me details of Mobile when you get them. Will call you later."

While Virginia stirred spices into her sauce, Wren furrowed her brow. *What could Virginia know that didn't seem noteworthy to her?*

"You mentioned that you overheard Chester and Philip talking about their Chattanooga business. What was it?" Wren asked.

"It was hard to tell because they were talking about a movie or a TV series about crime and a narcotics investigator, which caught my attention because I love crime books and movies. I didn't even realize they'd changed topics until Chester said something about dumping dead weight, and Philip told him that didn't have anything to do with their business in Chattanooga except it would take away their best location for production and their boss might think Chester was a liability. They got into an argument, and Chester said the boss didn't get all that involved in the business. I was a little surprised to hear that they were business associates because both of them struck me as being loners."

"I had that impression too."

"Wouldn't garlic knots be good with spaghetti? I have some in the freezer." Virginia pulled out the bread from the freezer and put it into the refrigerator to thaw then searched the refrigerator.

"I don't have any parmesan cheese." She exhaled. "I'll need to come up with something besides spaghetti; Samuel loves parmesan on his spaghetti."

"Shall I run to the store? It won't take long."

"No, I'll figure out ..."

Wren interrupted. "Shall I get a wedge?"

"That would be perfect, Wren."

When Wren picked up her jacket and her backpack, Rascal trotted to the back door. When Jack and Brandy followed him, he yipped, and their heads drooped.

"Sorry puppies, but I need you here to guard me," Virginia said.

Jack and Brandy pranced to Virginia and sat. She chuckled and gave them treats then hurried to Rascal and gave him a treat too.

"Text me if you think of anything else," Wren said as they left.

On the way to Dearheart, Wren said, "I didn't expect to hear from Charlie before tomorrow, but it certainly would have been nice if he'd called yesterday, so we'd be packing for our next campground tonight."

Rascal yipped then grinned.

Wren chuckled. "I'm not sure what I said either."

When Wren went into the grocery store, she stared at the varieties of parmesan cheese in the deli case.

"What would you like?"

"Do you know what kind of parmesan cheese Virginia Hudson likes?"

"Sure do; you want her usual?"

"Yes, please."

Wren gazed at the large wedge the clerk weighed then wrapped before she offered it to Wren.

"Anything else?" the clerk smiled as Wren accepted the wrapped package.

"That's it; thank you." Wren turned to leave, but Trooper Benson was standing close behind her; she stopped short before she bumped into him.

"Thought it was you," he said. "From the look of your purchase, you're doing the shopping for the Hudson family now. I didn't think writers could make enough money to live on. It was good of them to take you in, wasn't it?"

Wren crossed her arms and glared at him until he fidgeted and walked away.

An elderly woman stood next to Wren. "Good for you, dear. I was ready to run him down with my shopping cart, but you mowed him down just fine with one look; your mama would be proud."

Wren smiled. "Thank you."

After Wren climbed into the truck with Rascal, her phone rang.

When she answered, Dana Grace said, "I talked to Aunt Virginia. She said you were going into town; are you near the campground?"

"I'm at the grocery store; is there something you need at the campground?"

"I thought my wedding ring was in my purse, but I just remembered I left it next to the sink in my trailer, and I don't remember locking my trailer. I'm worried it might be stolen."

"I can check that real easy; I'll stop at the campground on the way back. I have a question for you that's been bothering me. When we were at the campground, and you were returning from the restroom, Trooper Benson said something to you. It was obvious it irritated you; what was it?"

"He told me respectable young ladies needed to realize what it looked like when they were alone without the protection of a man. I wanted to flash my pistol or maybe remove his big toe with a single shot then claim I had a hair trigger and a broken fingernail, so I missed where I meant to aim, but I was afraid Max would find out."

Wren snorted. "So Trooper Benson was under the protection of a man."

Dana Grace giggled. "I didn't think about that; I feel better."

After she hung up, Wren glanced at the sky as she headed toward the campground. "It might be close to dark before we return to the Hudsons', but Ghost said we shouldn't be on the road at night, so maybe twilight will be okay."

Rascal growled.

"I might be right; you don't know," Wren grumbled.

When Wren reached the campground, she slowly weaved around the deeper ruts as she made her way to Dana Grace's trailer.

While Rascal waited in the truck, Wren used the flashlight on her phone when she held her breath then went inside Dana Grace's dark trailer. The ring was next to the sink where Dana Grace had said. Wren picked it up then dropped it into the tiny watch pocket on her jeans.

After she was out of the trailer, she inhaled the fresh air and sent Dana Grace a text. "Got it."

Ghost said, "You gotta keep low, doll; nobody but you has the inside scoop."

The tone of his voice sent chills down her back. *He's right.* Wren glanced toward her truck. *No Ghost.* She jumped into her pickup and ignored the bumps and rolls as she rushed to the campground exit.

"We need to get to Virginia's house as fast as we can, Rascal; hang on."

As she hurried toward the Hudsons', the pungent odor of sour mash mixed with gasoline wafted from the back seat. She glanced at the backseat. *Ghost!*

"What are you doing here?" she asked.

"You got a punk on your tail who thinks you're an easy mark to bump off, doll."

She stared in the rearview mirror at the headlights of a car that was bearing down on her.

Ghost said, "They're going to try an old trick. Just do as I say, doll, and you'll be fine. Floor it; we want him at max speed."

"There's a hairpin curve not too far ahead."

"That's what he's counting on. What do you know about what to do in a skid?"

"Steer in the direction of the skid; so if the back of the pickup is going toward the right, I'd turn the steering wheel toward the right."

"You got it, doll; the trick is to fine tune it and not turn too much. What about a curve? How do you take a curve?"

"Not too fast."

"What if you're going fast, maybe too fast, into a curve?"

"I'd try to slow down."

"That won't work for you. This is what he thinks he's gonna do: as you get closer to the curve, he's going to try to catch up with you then right before you hit the curve, he'll give you a little love tap on your bumper. While you're fighting the skid and the curve, a chump will step onto the shoulder and throw something big at your truck to break your concentration, then your truck will go off the road and into the ravine."

"What do I do to mess them up?" Wren gritted her teeth.

"Atta girl. I'll talk you through it; just do what I say."

While Wren kept the accelerator pushed to the floorboard, Ghost said, "Hold tight onto the steering wheel; we don't want it to get away from you when he taps you."

When the curve ahead sign appeared, the car behind her was inches from her bumper.

Ghost said, "Ease up a little on the gas. We want to pick when and where he hits you. Here's your trick: keep your eyes on where you want to go, and that's where you'll steer. The curve goes to the right, so don't you be looking at the edge that drops off; look as far ahead as you can at the right side of the road. When he hits you, keep your tires straight then find your point again on the right and accelerate through the curve."

Wren voice cracked. "You make it sound easy."

"I've flipped into the ravine once, doll; it ain't gonna happen again."

Wren swallowed then nodded.

"Ease up a little more," Ghost said.

Wren slowed and was jolted by a bump on her rear bumper; she clutched the steering wheel and fought to keep her tires straight.

"Right side of the road," she mumbled to keep her focus on the farthest point on the right.

"He didn't realize you'd slowed down; we've put him on edge. The next one's going to be the real deal, but it will be rushed and careless. Slow down a little more."

Ghost chuckled as he turned to examine the car behind them. "I read you like a book, big shot."

He turned back and put one hand at the twelve o'clock position on the steering wheel. "Okay, doll, punch it."

Wren slammed her right foot down on the accelerator as hard as she could and held it in place.

"Keep watching that right side."

Wren glanced left out of the corner of her eye and gasped at the narrow shoulder and the long drop on the other side of the shoulder.

"Eyes right, doll."

Wren's pickup skidded. "Eyes right; tires straight."

"Loosen up on the steering wheel; I got it," Ghost said. "Now ease up on the gas."

As the pickup skidded toward the drop-off, Ghost said, "Let go of the steering wheel; slam hard on the accelerator then ease up."

Ghost whipped the steering wheel. "Slam it again."

The pickup whirled around in a donut while the car whizzed past them.

"Take your foot off the gas and brake to a smooth stop," Ghost said.

The car careened off the shoulder in front of them then teetered at the edge of the drop off.

Wren's eyes widened as the driver threw open his door. "Philip?"

The momentum of the swinging door tipped the car forward; as it dropped over the side and into the ravine before he could get out, Philip screamed, "Boss!"

Wren covered her ears with her hands at the terrifying sounds of Philip's screams and the metallic clangs and crunches of the car as it bounced off the trees and rocks on its way down to its final crash.

The deadly silence except for the startled call of crows added to her horror. Wren stared at the space where Philip's car had been and hyperventilated.

Chapter Sixteen

"Get a grip, doll; you gotta get out of here," Ghost said. "The man at the curve is on his way."

Wren's hands were shaking.

Ghost said, "You done good, but you gotta keep it together a little longer; I'm real sorry we don't have any 'shine to relax your nerves. Dog's fine."

After Wren turned around in the middle of the road with Ghost's help, she called the sheriff as she sped away.

Her voice shook as she said, "Philip tried to run me off the road, but he went over an embankment. I'm headed toward the campground; someone might be following me."

"Whoa, Wren. I didn't understand you."

Wren inhaled then slowly exhaled. "I'm on the road between the Hudsons' and the campground. Philip went into the ravine in his car after trying to ram my truck. I'm headed toward the campground, but Philip's partner might be following me."

"Got it; drive safely. I'll meet you at the campground in five minutes."

When she reached the campground, the sheriff was waiting in front of the office.

Wren turned to thank Ghost, but he was gone.

"Thank you," she whispered.

His voice carried from the raceway as he chuckled. "Don't mention it, doll."

Wren smiled. *Justin will laugh at Ghost's joke.*

While the sheriff examined the back of her pickup, Wren asked Rascal, "Are you okay?"

When Rascal grinned, Wren exhaled. "I am too."

Wren and Rascal joined the sheriff.

"I think it's mostly cosmetic damage, but it's hard to say. You'll need a new bumper because that's what they do these days, and you'll want a new hitch. You'll want to get it looked at before you hitch up another trailer. What about you and Rascal? Any injuries?"

"We're fine."

Wren told the sheriff about Philip chasing her and bumping into her then going over the edge into the ravine.

"Sounds like you did some pretty skillful driving there, Wren."

"Someone once told me to keep my eyes focused on where I wanted to go; it was hard, but I kept telling myself 'eyes right' because the drop off was on my left."

"You said someone was chasing you. Who was it?"

"I don't know; it was just a feeling."

"Where did Philip crash?"

"At one of the hairpin curves between here and the Hudsons'. I'm going back, so I could show you."

"Okay, let's do that."

The sheriff followed Wren; when she stopped and pointed, the sheriff shined his flashlight on the road. "Did you do a donut in the middle of the road?"

"I don't know; I was terrified and just trying to keep from going over the edge."

"Fear's a powerful motivator, isn't it? You can go on to the Hudsons'. If I have any more questions, I'll let you know."

When Wren arrived at the Hudsons', Dana Grace met her as she parked.

"I just got here too; thanks for letting me know you found my ring."

Wren pulled out the ring from her jeans pocket. "Here you go."

Dana Grace sighed. "I'll be glad when Max and I are settled and officially, publicly married. Are you okay, Wren? You seem a little quiet."

"I had an incident on the road here, but I'm fine and so is Rascal. Is it okay if we talk about it later?"

"Right after we eat?"

"I need to talk to Justin first."

"Okay, but that makes it sound even worse, so don't say anything to Aunt Virginia."

When the three of them went inside the house, Jack and Brandy rushed to greet Rascal.

"Let's run off some energy." Samuel followed the puppies as they raced after Rascal when he wheeled around and dashed across the yard.

"Do I have time to call Justin?" Wren asked.

"Take all the time you need; we won't see Samuel for a while, so there's no rush," Virginia said.

Wren hurried to her room.

When Justin answered, she said, "Ghost gave me a driving lesson."

"Why does that absolutely terrify me? I need to sit down, don't I?"

"It might be a good idea." Wren told him about the car chasing her, Ghost, and Philip going into the ravine.

"Wow; you and Ghost did a donut on a narrow, two-lane, mountain road at a hairpin curve with no shoulder to speak of to get out of the way of the bad guy who went into the ravine."

"That's a pretty good summary," Wren said.

"Ghost must have been a remarkable driver."

"He had so much confidence in what he was doing and in what he was telling me to do that I knew Rascal and I would be okay."

"Why was Philip trying to knock you off the road and into the ravine?" Justin asked.

"I think he and Chester were in the business of making and selling methamphetamines at the raceway concession stand. I saw some equipment and other paraphernalia there, but I didn't know what it was. I snapped photos at the concession stand and sent them to the sheriff."

"Was it active when you saw it?"

"I don't have any reference for that, so I'm not sure. I would have said no, except for a conversation that Virginia overheard," Wren said. "She heard Chester and Philip arguing at the gas station about a crime, except she thought they were talking about a movie. From what Virginia overheard, there is a third partner, who is the boss, according to Philip. The problem is that I've heard three or four people referred to as boss since I've been here."

"What about your truck? What kind of damage did Philip do when he rammed you?"

"The rear bumper's a little messed up, but the sheriff thinks it's mostly cosmetic; he said I should get the hitch looked at when I get to Mobile."

"Is there any way you can leave Dearheart tomorrow?"

Wren bit her lip. "I need to pack, and I'm still a little shaky, but I could try."

"Never mind; it was a bad idea. Just do me a favor and stay away from everyone that's been call the boss."

Wren chuckled. "Right off the top of my head, that includes Samuel, the librarian, and me."

Justin sighed. "Okay, those three are exempt."

Wren heard Samuel and the dogs come inside. Samuel said, "I'll feed the dogs; when do we eat?"

Wren said, "Our supper's ready; I'll let you know if anything changes."

"I love you, sweetie. Call me before you go to bed."

When Wren went into the kitchen, Dana Grace was setting the table while Virginia dished up spaghetti, and Samuel fed the dogs.

"We have parmesan to go with our spaghetti, thanks to Wren." Virginia pulled out the toasted garlic knots from the oven.

Wren set the grated parmesan cheese on the table, then everyone sat at their places.

After everyone had eaten and cleared the table, Virginia pointed to a towel that was covering a pie pan on the counter. "We have warm apple pie for dessert. Now or later?"

"I'm always ready for pie," Samuel said. "I brought home a couple of bottles of apple brandy that are just a shade above legal. The sheriff called me and told me to make sure Wren didn't leave the house tonight; I figured a sip or two of our best moonshine would do the trick."

Wren giggled. *Ghost told me I needed some 'shine for my nerves.*

While Virginia dished up pie into bowls, Wren scooped ice cream on top of each serving, and Dana Grace poured moonshine into juice glasses while Samuel took Rascal and the puppies outside.

When Samuel and the dogs came inside, Virginia said, "Let's be fancy and take our dessert into the living room."

After everyone was comfortably seated in the living room, and the dogs were settled on the rug, Dana Grace said, "Wren owes us a story."

Wren nodded then took a tiny sip of her apple brandy, which immediately took away her breath.

"Wow," she squeaked.

"Good stuff, isn't it? You were smart to sample it first," Samuel said.

Wren nodded then took a bite of ice cream to cool her throat. In between bites of pie and melted ice cream, Wren told them about Philip trying to run her off the road but instead losing control of his car and going into the ravine.

Virginia put her hand on her chest. "That's horrible. I guess having a pickup truck that was heavier and more stable than a car saved you, didn't it?"

"That and good driving," Samuel said. "Where'd you learn to drive like that?"

"I once did an article about a stock car crew; their driver gave me pointers when I drove one of their older cars around the track."

Rascal opened his eyes and stared at Wren then closed them.

She took another bite of pie and ice cream and a sip of apple brandy. *Best I could come up with on short notice.*

"Sounds like you've had great experiences as a freelance journalist," Dana Grace said. "Do you think you'll be able to settle down in one spot?"

"It's been fun traveling around, but I'm ready to put down some roots, and I'm enjoying the switch to fiction."

"When do you think you'll have your novel finished?" Virginia asked.

"I haven't put much time into it. After I have the fourth and last article behind me, I can start focusing on 'The High Falutin' Killer'."

"I talked to Lorinda today about the campground," Samuel said.

After Wren climbed into bed, she texted Betsy. "I heard from Charlie. My next stop is Lost Pirate Campground in Sirens Beach, Florida."

Betsy replied, "Call me?"

Wren smiled as she called Betsy. *No surprise.*

When Betsy answered, she asked, "This is your last article, right? Does that mean you'll be back in two weeks?"

"Something like that; how are you doing?" Wren asked.

"Much better because Socorro was released from what she called house arrest. Have you talked to Justin today? Terry is officially gone. The wife of the head of the school board ran into Terry in the grocery store yesterday and asked Terry if she was getting settled in. Terry told the nicest person in town that she couldn't wait to be out of Hidden Gulch, and that kind lady helped her out." Betsy chuckled. "Literally."

"What does that mean as far as the school is concerned? Are they still short a teacher?"

"Yes, but they have our committee's recommendation for a more efficient hiring process that doesn't involve us. Just a second, Butch wants to tell me something."

A few seconds later, Betsy asked, "Is it your bedtime there? Am I keeping you up?"

"I just climbed into bed, but I wanted to let you know about Florida."

"That's really great news; get some rest, and let me know if anything changes."

After she hung up, Wren called Justin. When he answered, she said, "Tell me about your day."

Justin chuckled. "I hope that means that there's nothing new in Tennessee."

"That's exactly right; I talked to Betsy, and she told me about Terry."

"That was actually the newsflash of the day. It was great from my point of view because I got a lot of work done while the rest of the town was in an uproar."

Justin cleared his throat. "If I got a really good deal on a fifth wheel that we would like, would you want to look at it before I bought it?"

"No, you don't need my approval to buy a fifth wheel."

"Yes, I do because I am not going camping alone."

Wren was silent.

"Wren? Are we okay?" Justin asked.

"I thought we were going camping like sometime later next year, so you wouldn't need to buy a fifth wheel now."

"Are you thinking about privacy? Because you'd have the bedroom, and I'll have the spare bed."

"You're too tall to sleep on one of the uncomfortable fold-out beds in a fifth wheel."

"Nope, the foldouts are actually comfortable now; I've been reading the reviews."

"I should sleep on the foldout bed; in case you haven't noticed, I'm not tall."

"But if it's a matter of privacy..."

Wren interrupted. "I'll sleep in my modest long johns."

"Okay, so we'll figure all that out, right? Back to my question."

"No, I don't have to look at it, but send me a link, so I can check the reviews myself."

Justin chuckled. "Fair enough. I have another question for you: if we're traveling with my fifth wheel, do you want to be the driver, the navigator, or switch off?"

"I'd be okay with switching off, but I'd prefer to be the navigator, especially if we pick up paper maps from the welcome stations at state lines."

"You read paper maps? That's awesome, so do I. It's like Survival 101, isn't it? Where would you like to go first if I have a week off for vacation?"

"I'd like to explore Arizona. Where would you like to go?"

"Only a week? I think exploring Arizona is a great idea. We'll have to research to see what sounds interesting then plan our route."

"I love it; planning is half the fun." Wren yawned.

"Honey, I know you must be exhausted. We'll talk more tomorrow; I love you."

Chapter Seventeen

Wren gasped and sat up in bed with a start; she was damp with sweat and breathing hard. She glanced around the dark room then stared at her phone. *Three o'clock.*

Rascal trotted to her bedside and whined. Wren exhaled and stroked his ears and back. "I had a nightmare; we were in my truck and we went over a cliff."

After her breathing returned to normal, Rascal laid down near the door, and Wren closed her eyes and relaxed. *We're okay.*

Wren woke to whining puppies and the aroma of coffee.

"Shhh," Virginia whispered. "You're going to wake everybody up. Let me grab my coat, then we can go out."

Wren followed Rascal to the kitchen.

"Did we wake you up?" Virginia asked.

"It's my usual time to get up, and I smelled coffee."

"We'll be back in a few minutes; I wanted a turn with the puppies." Virginia opened the crates, and Jack and Brandy darted to the back door.

"Help yourself to the coffee." Virginia opened the door and followed the puppies and Rascal outside.

Wren checked her phone and found a text from Justin.

"Here's the link. Let me know what you think."

Wren poured a cup of coffee then sat at the table as she tapped the link. She raised her eyebrows. *This isn't bad at all.*

After she carefully examined the layout, Wren searched for reviews and read them.

She replied, "I like it. What type of hitch were you thinking about?"

Wren carried her cup to her room to dress while she drained her cup. When she returned to the kitchen, Dana Grace was dressed as she sat at the table with her hands wrapped around her cup.

"I heard from Max this morning; he'll be here this weekend. I'm sorry you won't be able to meet him. You're leaving in the morning, right?"

Samuel, Virginia, and the dogs came in the back door.

"We got caught outside; it's downright nippy out there," Virginia said. "I was planning blueberry pancakes for breakfast this morning; is that okay with everyone?"

"Sounds good to me," Samuel said. "Shall I fry up a mess of bacon?"

"That's perfect; I'll feed the dogs, so you can monopolize the stove. Anybody want eggs with your bacon and pancakes?"

Dana Grace and Wren shook their heads.

After breakfast, Samuel and Dana Grace left in Samuel's truck for the apple orchard.

Wren's phone rang.

When she answered it, Lilibeth said, "Ruth Whitaker called me; she just heard that you were leaving tomorrow, is that right?"

Wren smiled. *News gets around.* "First thing."

"Will you have time to come to the library this morning? I have paperwork to finish before I open the doors for our patrons, and she wants to be here at nine o'clock to chat with you without being interrupted. Can you be here about the same time?"

"We'll see you at nine."

After she hung up, Wren said, "Rascal and I are going to the library this morning to talk to Ruth Whitaker; do you need anything from town?"

"I'll look over my list, but I can't think of anything that can't wait until my weekly trip."

Wren turned on her computer to check email and write while Virginia sat at the table with her book and notebook.

Wren stretched a little after eight. "I'll finish up this paragraph then get ready to go into town."

Wren straightened her room before she took a quick shower. She put on a long-sleeved flannel shirt over her T-shirt but didn't tuck it into her jeans. After she brushed her hair and her teeth, she patted her waist where her pistol rode then picked up her backpack and jacket as she headed to the back door.

"I'm going to the library, Rascal; are you going with me?"

Rascal followed Wren to the door.

"Do you expect to be back before lunch?" Virginia asked.

"I would think so; I'll let you know if that changes."

When they went outside, Wren exhaled. "It's so cold, I can see my breath."

She rushed to the truck; after Rascal was in the backseat, she hopped in and turned on the engine. The fan blew cold air, and Wren shivered. "Warm up, truck. I should stick my gloves into my jacket pockets. It's cold in the mountains, isn't it, Rascal?"

When she was halfway to town, the heater kicked in and the vents blew warm air into the cab of her truck. "That feels good, doesn't it?"

Wren pulled into the gas station. "I'll fill up now for tomorrow morning; we have time."

While Wren stood next to the pump as she filled the tank, a woman drove past her toward the store. The woman smiled and waved; after she parked in front of the store, she called out, "We'll miss you, Wren, but my friends and I have signed up for your blog, so we can keep in touch."

"Thank you," Wren said.

On the way to the library, Wren said, "I just needed a little time to become a local, didn't I?"

When she turned to enter the library parking lot, Ghost asked, "Are you here for the ambush?"

She jerked her head and squinted at Ghost, who sat in the passenger's seat.

"Ambush? No, I'm here to talk to Ruth Whitaker."

"She's my niece." Ghost chuckled. "She always called me Uncle Ghost, but about that ambush...we need a little strategy session. Park over there away from the building as close to the woods as you can get."

After Wren parked, Ghost said, "You carry a piece; how good of a shot are you?"

"Pretty good," Wren said.

Ghost snorted. "Well, that won't cut it one bit."

"I'm pretty darn good and never miss," Wren growled.

"Okay, doll, this is the plan: you have to leave the library before nine thirty."

Ghost turned to Rascal. "When you come out of the library, dog, start barking and run to the woods. Growl mean-like if you see a man in the woods. If you don't see a man get real quiet and watch doll from the trees. Start barking as soon as you see a man turn the corner of the library because that's how he plans to ambush her."

Ghost turned back to Wren. "You be ready to shoot when dog starts barking, and by ready to shoot, I mean have that pistol out of its holster. If there's a change in the killer's plan, I'll let you know."

"You got it, Rascal?" Wren asked.

Rascal grinned.

Wren furrowed her brow. "What if we just drive away now?"

"He'll ambush you somewhere else. Right here before nine thirty is perfect because we won't have any people around who could get hit by crossfire."

"Makes sense to me; we just need for him to play his part right. I don't suppose he'll just go away."

Ghost chuckled. "Sure, doll. You write that in your story."

Wren sighed. "Good point."

After she climbed out of the truck, she removed her coat and tossed it onto her seat before she opened the back door for

Rascal. *I'll be less encumbered when I come out of the library if I don't have my coat.*

The library door was locked; Wren shivered and knocked. *Bad idea. I can't shiver and shoot.* She raced back to her truck and put on her jacket as Lilibeth opened the door.

"Did you run back for your coat?" Lilibeth asked.

"Sure did; the truck got warm, so I took it off. I forgot for a second there why I wore it in the first place."

Lilibeth smiled. "It feels extra cold this morning, doesn't it? Ruth is waiting for you in the conference room."

Wren and Rascal followed Lilibeth.

When they went into the room, Ruth Whitaker sat at the head of the table.

Wren said, "Good morning, Miss Ruth."

"It's real nice of you to come see me before you leave town."

Wren sat down next to Ruth, who put her hands on the table.

"Put your hands on mine, Wren. I want to feel the connection."

Wren put her hands on top of Miss Ruth's and felt Ghost behind her. *I wonder if Miss Ruth feels Ghost here too.*

"I had a little more to tell you about Uncle Ghost." Miss Ruth's sightless eyes stared toward the ceiling.

"He had a girlfriend." Miss Ruth pulled back one of her hands and waved it as though she was shooing away a pesky fly from her ear. "Not a romantic girlfriend; more like a best friend. I don't even know her name; he called her Doll. Norman Hudson and his boys were putting a lot of pressure on Clarence Whitaker to let them partner in his business and it got to the point where they were threatening him. They told Uncle Ghost he should drive for them, so Doll wouldn't get hurt. Uncle Ghost told Clarence what they said, but Clarence said they were full of hot air. One afternoon, Doll just up and disappeared. Uncle Ghost was frantic because he was certain the Hudsons had taken her. On his run that night, the Hudsons waited for him on his usual route. They pulled up their car behind him then knocked the rear of his car to make him skid and go into the ravine, but he was a far better driver than they were. As Uncle Ghost was pulling away from them, one of their henchmen pushed Doll into the road. Uncle Ghost had two choices: hit Doll or take his chances going into the ravine. He didn't survive."

When Miss Ruth's voice cracked, Wren patted her hand.

Miss Ruth continued, "Doll grabbed the gun from the Hudson thug who had pushed her in front of Uncle Ghost and shot him then kicked him into the ravine. She went straight to Clarence and told him what happened and left the mountain. We never knew where she went, but she was related to the Williams. I just wanted you to know."

Wren glanced at the clock on the wall. *Nine twenty.*

"Thank you, Miss Ruth; I appreciate the story more than you could imagine."

Miss Ruth nodded. "I didn't want the story to die with me. Tell the story someday, please."

"I will." A tear slipped down Wren's face. "I have to go."

"Yes, be safe; give the killer a taste of lead for me."

"I will."

When Wren rose from her chair, Ghost whispered, "No change."

After Wren and Rascal reached the front door, Wren frowned. *My coat's too bulky.* She pulled off her coat then removed her pistol from its holster before she and Rascal went outside. She dropped her jacket next to the door; Rascal barked and continued barking as he raced to the trees then became quiet.

"Okay, doll. Keep your eyes on the target. You can let him shoot first because his shot will go wide when dog barks. Take him down."

Wren heard a car pull into the parking lot. *Eyes on target.*

A man rounded the corner with a pistol in his hand as he aimed at Wren, Rascal barked, and Wren fired.

"Down!" Ghost shouted and shoved Wren to the ground as a second shot fired from behind her.

"Roll and fire," Ghost ordered.

Wren rolled over and fired at the figure behind her who had aimed his gun at her head, and the second man dropped to the ground.

Rascal raced to Wren and stood next to her.

"You aren't hit, are you, doll?"

"No," she growled.

Sirens sounded nearby.

"You're about to have company, doll."

"I have to see who the men are who shot at me." Wren struggled to her feet.

Ghost took her elbow to steady her. "You'll know soon enough."

"Come on; I need to know." Wren took a step and winced. "Dang it; I've reinjured my ankle."

"Just adds to your delicate, killer image," Ghost chuckled. "Cops are here; good job, doll. You're a pretty good shot."

Ghost disappeared, and Wren dropped to her knee when her ankle gave way.

A deputy raced to Wren and helped her up. "Are you okay, Wren? Did you get caught in the crossfire?"

Wren's mouth quivered, and she bit her lip to keep away the smile. *I like that version: two bad guys shot each other when they tried to shoot me. Maybe I'll try it out on the sheriff.*

Wren shivered. "My coat's by the library door. Would you mind getting it for me?"

While the deputy raced to the library door for her coat, she gritted her teeth as she put a little weight on her ankle. After the deputy helped her with her coat, the sheriff arrived, and Rascal wagged his tail.

"Check the other assailant, Deputy," the sheriff said. "What happened, Wren?"

"Would you believe I got caught in the crossfire?" she asked.

The sheriff narrowed his eyes. "No."

Wren shrugged. "The man next to the library came around the corner and shot at me, so I shot him; I fell as the man behind me fired, then I rolled and shot him. Who are they?"

The deputy returned and whispered to the sheriff, "Hank. Deceased."

"Check the library's security camera," the sheriff said.

"Who was the man behind me?" Wren asked. "I didn't see his face; all I saw was his gun pointed at my head, so I fired."

Sheriff narrowed his eyes. "Trooper Benson claims that Hank shot him."

"Are you going to take my gun for ballistics?"

"Might not have to; it depends on whether the library security camera was operational."

The deputy hurried to the sheriff and whispered, "You have to see this."

Wren covered her mouth to hide her smile. *He's whispering, but he knows I can hear him.*

"Can I go with you? It's cold out here," Wren said.

The sheriff rolled his eyes. "Hang onto my arm."

"I can help her, Sheriff," the deputy said.

"I need you to stay with Trooper Benson until the ambulance arrives. Record everything he says."

The deputy's smile drooped. "Yes, sir."

When they went into the library, Lilibeth asked, "Are you shot, Wren?"

"I twisted my ankle again."

"Oh, that's good; I mean, that's good you weren't shot. The camera feed is in my office, Sheriff. Wren, I have an extensive first aid box; shall I wrap your ankle for you?"

"That might help."

"I may have a brace too. You could probably use the extra support."

Lilibeth sat at a keyboard. "This is the video I have, sheriff. When I heard the first shot, I dashed in here and turned on the cameras. They're usually off during the day."

The video showed Wren with her pistol in her hand with it pointed to the ground. Rascal barked and a shot rang out, then Wren raised her pistol and fired. Trooper Benson stood behind Wren and aimed at her and fired as she fell; she rolled and returned his fire, and he went down.

Sheriff frowned. "I thought Lilibeth said she turned on the video when she heard a shot."

"Maybe it was already on, and she was confused," Wren said. *I wonder if Miss Ruth told her to turn it on.*

"I suppose; that's a really clear video, Wren. Why did you fall?" Sheriff asked.

"I don't know; maybe I was scared."

"Any normal person would have been." Sheriff turned off Lilibeth's security system and computer. "Except you," he mumbled.

"So Hank was the boss of the drug operation, wasn't he? Where did Benson fit in?" Wren asked.

Sheriff rose and closed the door. "I think he was making extra money, or maybe he was addicted and blackmailed into helping. That's up to the lawyers and the courts."

Lilibeth tapped on the door.

"Come on in, Lilibeth," the sheriff said.

Before he left, the sheriff added, "Call your marshal; I'll talk to him later."

After Lilibeth wrapped Wren's ankle and put on the brace, she said, "I'll close the door; it's a zoo out there right now. You're welcome to stay right here until it all settles down outside. It's been very exciting to have you with us, Wren."

Wren called Justin. When he answered, she said, "Hi, honey; I twisted my ankle again."

"I know you did, sweetheart; the sheriff's giving you a chance to call me before he does, isn't he?"

"You already know?"

"The deputy called me, but I'd love to hear your version."

"Ghost helped me."

"I knew he had to be there. Are you still leaving tomorrow morning for Mobile?"

"That's my plan."

"Mine too; I love you, Wren."

Wren smiled after they hung up. *I need to tell him about my wonderful boyfriend.*

Next to read:

SLAUGHTERED IN THE SAND

WREN AND RASCAL COZY MYSTERY, BOOK 4

Wren's fourth and final writing assignment: a haunted campground near a Florida beach.

Wren and Rascal, her protective Labrador Retriever, arrive at a nearly abandoned, neglected campground. Wren discovers clues to a cold case in old letters. Are the new murders related?

The ghostly pirate Captain warns Wren of danger; the killer plans Wren's untimely demise.

How's it going with Justin, the Arizona town Marshal? "This relationship stuff is hard..." ~ Wren

Acknowledgements

Huge thanks to my husband for his patience, support, talented technical expertise, and guidance.

Thanks to my editor, family, friends, and faithful readers for their awesome support and encouragement.

Thank you for reading. You keep reading; I'll keep writing!

Tell a friend how much you love Wren and Rascal and leave a short review with Barrett Book Shop or your favorite retailer. Authors can always use a few sparkles to brighten the gloomiest days.

PRO TIP: Post a five-star rating or recommend a book: both count the same as reviews!

Ready for news about what's next?

Look for the NEWSLETTER tab on JUDITHABARRETT.COM to subscribe to my not-your-typical newsletter for stories, new releases, and VIP Reader bargains!

About the Author

Judith A. Barrett, award-winning author, lives on a farm in Georgia with her husband, two dogs, and chickens. She writes series for her readers: thriller, mystery, post-apocalyptic science fiction, and cozy mystery novels. Stories with a twist: not your typical characters from not your typical author!

When she isn't writing, Judith is working on farm chores, hiking or camping with her husband and dogs, or rocking on her front porch while she watches the sunset.

You keep reading; I'll keep writing!

Website www.judithabarrett.com
Subscribe to her eNewsletter via her website

BARRETT BOOK SHOP
Browse, shop, read, enjoy!
EXCLUSIVE! Buy your next paperback book from the author and receive your personalized Signed by the Author copy!

www.ingramcontent.com/pod-product-compliance
Lightning Source LLC
Chambersburg PA
CBHW070219030726
47505CB00006B/1737